ELECTRIC DRAGON

Dushma hurried across the landing, the floorboards rattling. Then halfway across she froze. *What if they were waiting for her on the stairs?*

As she hesitated, a tiny noise nearby made her turn her head. She was standing opposite the entrance to the derelict flat next door to her own. At first it seemed untouched, but as she looked more closely she noticed fresh scratches in the wood of the jamb next to the lock. Then she heard the noise again: a faint squeak like a rusty bicycle, or…

Almost imperceptibly, the handle was turning.

Also by Patrick Wood

The Fireglass Machine

Point

ELECTRIC DRAGON

PATRICK WOOD

■SCHOLASTIC

Scholastic Children's Books,
Commonwealth House, 1-19 New Oxford Street,
London, WC1A 1NU, UK
a division of Scholastic Ltd
London ~ New York ~ Toronto ~ Sydney ~ Auckland
Mexico City ~ New Delhi ~ Hong Kong

First published by Scholastic Ltd as
Viaduct Child, 2002

This edition published by Scholastic Ltd, 2005

Copyright © Patrick Wood, 2002

Cover illustration copyright © David Wyatt, 2005

ISBN 0 439 96389 3

Printed by Nørhaven Paperback A/S, Denmark

10 9 8 7 6 5 4 3 2 1

PART
I

I

Dushma shuffled closer to the window. She could feel the man behind her swaying with impatience. The soles of his shoes scraped against the gritty tiles and his flapping coat brushed the back of her skirt.

She looked up at the arched ceiling and then deliberately down at her clenched knuckles, trying to resist the urge to glance back over her shoulder. She knew instinctively that such a gesture would mark her out: the sudden moist flash of dark pupils in the whites of her wide and frightened eyes.

A loudspeaker announcement rolled around the ticket hall, incomprehensible to Dushma. She concentrated, sure the message must be to do with her, but the announcer had the microphone wrongly positioned and the rustle of papers on his desk was louder than his voice. No one else seemed even to be trying to listen. She gave up and turned her attention instead to a list of fares stuck to an adjacent wall.

Her only thought when she entered the station had been

to get off the street, and she still had no idea where she was going. There was no map near where she stood. So as not to appear suspicious, she tried to hear what destinations the people around her were requesting, but the echoes in the busy ticket hall blurred their speech. Nothing she could catch made any sense to her.

"I dunno…" the woman at the next window was saying listlessly. "I dunno, 'f I want sour feelin' … or no feelin'…"

The man in front of Dushma scooped up his change, stooped to seize his briefcase from between his feet and then, still crouching, loped away from the ticket window. It was her turn. She put her fists up on the cold metal sill, feeling the coins slippery and hot in her clammy palm.

"Three stops please," she said, hoping she didn't need to be any more specific.

The assistant didn't look at her, but kept on stacking money in the slots and tubes inside his till. "You got your ID card?"

This was the moment she had dreaded. She feigned surprise, pushed a hand hurriedly into one pocket, then fumbled inside her coat. Affecting exasperation, she rolled her eyes and shrugged. Resignedly, she unslung her satchel from her shoulder. *All right*, she seemed to say, *if you honestly want to stand there and watch me sift through my possessions…*

The assistant began sliding her money towards him through the slot below the thick glass of his protective window. "Bring your ID next time. Polite or impolite?"

This time she really was taken unawares. "I… What?"

"Oh, come on!" hissed the man behind her, as if to himself but clearly intending them both to hear.

The assistant punched some buttons and a long orange ticket lolled out of the slot by Dushma's right hand. She grabbed at it and tore it free, feeling the perforations give like the stiff zipper on a brand new jacket.

A sense of exhilaration overcame her as she rushed down the long escalator towards the platforms, her satchel bumping on her hip. Her earlier panic disappeared, drowned in the excitement of being out on her own in a place she'd never been before. She'd succeeded at the ticket booth, she could find her way around, she could go anywhere! Nobody could catch her now...

Hemispherical lights on iron poles shone a warm yellow glow on the curved brick ceiling overhead. A hot breeze blew past her, billowing out her filmy scarf and stinging her eyes. Weaving her way past the other people on the escalator, Dushma felt the pins and grips beginning to lose their hold on her thick, dark hair. Recklessly she snaked herself around protruding elbows and leapt over bags she found in her path, clutching for balance at the moving rubber handrail.

The wind grew stronger as she reached the platform and squirmed through the waiting passengers. A sign creaked on its hinges above her head. The crowd thinned and in front of her she saw the bright gleam of track, lying in its concrete pit below the lip of the platform. The roar of an approaching train filled her ears.

She caught a zigzag movement in the corner of her eye. Leaning quickly forward she saw to her astonishment a tiny grey mouse running backwards and forwards beneath the rails. It seemed to move randomly, bouncing off obstacles and then gliding onwards as if on wheels. Then she flinched backwards again as the train burst out of the tunnel, pushing a wave of hot and dusty air before it.

Some of the carriages were orange and others were blue. Her orange ticket firmly in one hand, Dushma moved towards a door of the appropriate colour. The train had stopped but a rumbling noise continued in the distance. She wondered what labyrinthine tunnels ran above and below and alongside the one in which she stood.

By the time she had boarded the train all the seats had been taken. Hot from her run, she brushed damp strands of hair from her eyes and wrapped a dangling leather strap around her wrist to steady herself. There was no more space in either direction, but nevertheless men with briefcases held out in front of them like battering rams pushed their way past her, back and forth along the aisle.

"Minotaurs!" the driver shouted warningly, and the last few people on the platform hurried to squeeze themselves into the already crowded carriages before the doors hissed shut.

II

Dushma lived with her Auntie Megan high up in an arch of the railway viaduct. This huge brick structure crossed London from one side to the other, jammed like a giant comb teeth-first into the streets and squares and parks of the city. Express trains rushed across it night and day, clattering and whistling as they went.

No one was supposed to live in the viaduct. As far as Dushma and her aunt knew, no one else did. There was another set of rooms like theirs next door, but they almost never got the sun and so remained dusty and empty. Auntie Megan's theory was that these apartments had been meant as temporary accommodation for the navvies who worked on the viaduct, and when building was complete they had been forgotten. There was electricity and hot water, but they had never been sent a bill.

It was an interesting place to live, although it had its drawbacks. There was plenty of space, but the walls were mostly bare brick. Nor were there carpets in any of the rooms. "Loft living, isn't it?" said Auntie Megan sometimes, when in one of her carefree moods. "It's *supposed* to be minimalist. It's the height of chic!" But it could be painfully cold in the winter, despite Auntie Megan's attempts to make it cosier by stuffing old newspapers into the cracks between the floorboards and fitting pink-tinged light bulbs in all the sockets.

It was a long way up, too. They could see for miles from their windows. The only buildings at an equal height were the chimney stacks of factories and the dizzying central spire of St Gotha's Cathedral. But there was no lift, so to reach their front door they had to climb the thousands of steps of the wrought-iron spiral staircase that ran up inside one leg of the viaduct.

Within, their home was a curious shape. Their living-room wall, for example, curved right to the top of the inside of the arch. The highest window looked almost straight downwards. There was a grille to prevent people falling out when the window was open, although someone as thin as Dushma could probably squeeze through. But if she was careful she could lie across the bars, her arms dangling in space like a bushbaby on a bough, and look directly down into the huge, slowly rotating propeller of the underground railway ventilation shaft far below.

Mr Mackenzie, one of Auntie Megan's string-vested lodgers, once constructed a parachute for Dushma to launch from out of this window. For the canopy, he used a large white square of material from one of his old shirts.

Then he tied string to each corner and suspended a plastic soldier from it.

"Mmm, smell those sweaty armpits," he cackled, as they lay at the open window preparing for the drop. He was referring not to the remains of his shirt, but to the stale air he imagined being sucked up out of the underground railway tunnels by the giant fan at the foot of their arch. In fact, being so far above the traffic fumes, the breezes that blew past their flat were almost always sweet, except when an express went over the viaduct and invisible clouds of ozone rolled humming down from the electric rails.

"Will it tangle it up?" asked Dushma, holding the parachute ready and watching the hypnotic spin of the distant propeller blades beneath their wire-mesh covering.

"Wait and see," said Mr Mackenzie.

The parachute fluttered downwards, bright in the sunlight, spinning slowly and swooping from side to side until, about two thirds of the way to the ground, the updraught from the ventilation shaft cancelled out the force of gravity and it began to rise again. Dushma had been thrilled, sure that it would come all the way back up again like a slow-motion bungee jump. But instead it slid sideways out of the column of warm air and drifted out of sight.

"Ah, we should've attached a message to it," said Mr Mackenzie. "You know, telling people where to send it back to if they find it. Like people put in bottles, then they throw them in the sea. Who knows, it might end up in France, or anywhere!"

"That would've been a good idea," Dushma agreed. "Can you make another one?" But Mr Mackenzie said he had no more white shirts.

Mr Mackenzie was the strangest and most entertaining of Auntie Megan's string of string-vested lodgers, and it was with his sudden departure that everything had started to go so horribly wrong. Several of his predecessors had also been called Mr Mackenzie, or sometimes Mr MacHendry or something similar, leading Dushma to suspect as she grew older and less gullible that in fact none of them was called Mr Mackenzie, or whatever it was Auntie Megan introduced them as.

Most of them tended to lurk in the spare room throughout their stay, only emerging at mealtimes. At the table they would hardly speak at all except to give brief and reluctant answers to Auntie Megan's small talk. This latest Mr Mackenzie, however, had been much more communicative. He liked to surprise Dushma at odd hours of the day with a trick, an observation or an interesting piece of information.

"We'd be OK up here if there was a flood," he'd said to her one time when she'd been lying at the open living-room window. "We could get up on to the railway and escape to safety, couldn't we? Walk all the way to France, even!"

It was indeed possible for them to climb right out on to the viaduct. The landing outside their flat was little more than a wooden platform suspended in a lofty space, criss-crossed with dusty bars of sunlight in the summer from the many chinks in the brick. Pigeons got in sometimes, and flapped around in panic or sat burbling on a ledge.

A short vertical ladder led upwards from the landing to a manhole cover which opened on to the gravel verge of the railway line. Dushma sometimes climbed this ladder, raising the hinged metal lid above it just enough to see up and down the gleaming metal rails. Further than this she was strictly forbidden to go because, a few metres from the manhole cover, there stood a pole with a buzzing camera turning left and right on top of it. But if there had been a flood, of course, then there wouldn't be anybody watching.

The only other feature of the railway verge was a life raft suspended from davits, ready to be swung out over the side of the viaduct so that train-crash survivors could descend to safety. One evening, after drinking too much sherry and nearly setting light to herself with the aromatherapy burner, Auntie Megan had made a notice and stuck it to the front door. "In the event of fire or flood, man the lifeboat!" it said.

"Reminds me of night-time bombing raids in the war," confided Mr Mackenzie to Dushma, lying at the living-room window after dark with the lights turned off. "You're hanging there in this glass bubble in the belly of the plane," he explained, "looking for a shadow underneath you, waiting for the tracer bullets like a line of street lights in the distance when the enemy opens fire. Hoping you'll get it cleanly when it comes. Those things turn into flaming

11

coffins in an instant. No chance to climb back up inside and bale out the hatch. See these bars here? I could've hung from those when I was younger. What, five minutes, ten? Squeezing tennis balls, that's the secret."

Dushma didn't know whether to believe him or not, about the war or the bars. He looked quite old, with his grizzled stubble and slack, wrinkled skin. And his wrists were still thick and sinewy.

Throughout their acquaintance, Dushma would not see Mr Mackenzie lose his temper until the day he fell out with Auntie Megan and left for good. Before then she knew him only as the mildest of men. The only thing that annoyed him was the regular passage of the trains across the viaduct. "Makes my fillings rattle," he complained.

Once they were playing chess in the living room when the air began to hum and the walls to rumble with the vibration of an approaching express. It was a sensation Dushma had grown so used to that she hardly noticed it any more. But Mr Mackenzie jumped to his feet, reached into his pocket and took something out of his wallet. Just before the train passed overhead he extended his hand and opened his fingers, revealing a tiny silver needle in his palm. Then he lifted his arm up high and Dushma saw the needle rise towards the ceiling, hang trembling in mid-air, and then drop back as the train moved on.

"See!" he said triumphantly, as if he had proved something. "Living here all your life, I don't know why your hair's not all frizzed up like curly wire."

He never asked her anything about herself, like why she didn't go to school, or why her friends never came to visit. Dushma assumed that he knew at least some details of her situation and avoided such subjects out of tact. She had read somewhere that it used to be considered polite to ask people questions about themselves, to show you were interested in them. It used to be bad manners to talk too much about oneself. But now, she read, society had fragmented to such an extent that nobody could tell which questions would be welcome and which might be intrusive. So now, if you didn't really want to know, you shouldn't ask.

"What does it mean, society is fragmenting?" she had asked Auntie Megan.

"It means everybody's cracking up!" shrieked Auntie Megan, whooping with laughter at her joke and pouring herself another glass of sherry.

One of Dushma's most vivid early memories was of the tall fridge-freezer in the kitchen.

It had been bought only the previous week, paid for in long-hoarded wads of crumpled notes. Three strong men had taken all morning to carry it up the stairs. It was Auntie Megan's pride and joy, and meant they no longer had to hang their milk out of the window in carrier bags.

Dushma always woke early in the summer, when the uninterrupted sun streamed into her bedroom window through the thin curtains. She would get up and pad through into the kitchen, still in her nightie, and make herself breakfast.

A tangle of creeper or ivy had escaped the spray of the weedkiller trucks that ran along the railway every spring, and green fronds grew down around the kitchen window. Dushma enjoyed standing at the sink with the shadows of leaves swaying across her face. She liked to screw up her eyes and watch the sunlight oozing through the dusty bottles on the window sill and spraying off the gleaming taps.

But on this particular morning she went instead to the fridge, climbed up on to a stool and began to play with the set of magnets clustered on the door. There were letters, words and pictures, but she made no attempt to construct sentences or stories. Instead she simply slid the magnets over the surface of the fridge door, enjoying the sticky feel when she pulled them away, and the dry, flat snap they made on reattaching themselves.

She must have stood there for hours, arranging the magnets into different patterns, sometimes pausing and just standing there, leaning against the fridge, enjoying the feel of the cool metal against her cheek and the steady throb of its motor in her bones. Then Auntie Megan came in to make her morning cup of tea, shooed Dushma off the stool and pulled the fridge door open.

The inside of the fridge was solid with frost. The items it contained were almost unrecognizable under a thick fur of ice crystals. A cloud of condensation rolled out into the room and around the two of them, tingling against their skin and forming beads of moisture on their eyelashes. A flurry of snow drifted down to the floor.

Dushma backed away, sure that this would somehow turn out to be her fault. But at first Auntie Megan was too surprised to be cross. "Would you believe it?" she muttered to herself, reaching in to tug the milk free. "Was it you? Have you been fiddling with the dial?" The milk had frozen and expanded, bloating its cardboard carton.

Mutely Dushma shook her head.

"Well, anyway, you shouldn't… Maybe there was a power surge? Oh, look at this… I'll have to wait till it defrosts, it could take hours!" She banged the rock-like pint of milk down on the draining board. She was getting angry now. She could work herself up with extraordinary speed, especially on those mornings when she had a headache. Dushma moved further out of her reach.

"*Why* are you always such a nuisance? Any *normal* girl would've been at school instead of hanging around like a millstone round my neck. Yes, that's what you are, a bloody useless nuisance! I wish I'd never promised your mother I'd look after you, I really do. Too soft by far, that's my trouble. I could've had a life, got out of this dump. Well, it's too late now, but don't you worry, oh no, 'cos I've got plans for you, you wait and see! You'll make it worth my while eventually, I promise you!"

"I'm sorry," whispered Dushma, not sure what she had done. "I'll clean it up." Her voice was hoarse from the dryness in her mouth. She was not looking directly at Auntie Megan but staring past her at the open fridge and its smoking interior, clotted with frost.

"Oh, what's the use?" muttered Auntie Megan. "Just … just keep out of the way, will you?

Dushma fled back to her bedroom. She dressed quickly, then crouched down beside the head of her bed and pressed her ear against the wall to listen for a train. When she heard one approaching, she slipped back out into the corridor and, any noise she made masked by the clattering wheels overhead, ran out of the flat and down the spiral stairs into the hot and dusty mid-morning.

III

Dushma wasn't registered. This was a fact that she'd lived with for as long as she could remember. It meant, among other things, that she couldn't go to school, or see a doctor, or buy tickets to travel on public transport.

Instead of school she taught herself from an old edition of the *Encyclopaedia Britannica*, read novels left behind by various Mackenzies, and tried to learn how to play the guitar.

She couldn't catch a bus or a train, but she explored exhaustively on foot. The streets near where she lived were lined with office blocks, factories and fat brick chimneys seeping smoke. Off the main thoroughfares, narrow lanes ran this way and that between secretive walls, something interesting at the end of almost every one. There might be a school with a steeply gabled roof of bluish slate and a playground ringed with curly wrought-iron fencing. Or a warehouse with windows divided by strips of lead into multiple panes that gleamed or glowered according to the light.

By the time she was fourteen Dushma could have found her way blindfold down every cobbled alley in the neighbourhood. This was when she began to go further afield. She made herself sandwiches and walked as far as she could go and come back in a day. When it was cold she sat quietly in a pew at the back of a church, or hovered above the rising warmth of a bank of votive candles. She learned a lot of history by reading leaflets and posters, or simply asking people.

It was in this way that she heard about the great fire of 1871, and how London had been rebuilt entirely of bricks in splendid late-Victorian Gothic style. All the capital's most famous churches dated from around this time: St Klaed's, St Mungo's, St Elmo's ... and, most magnificent of all, the monstrous cathedral of St Gotha.

The cathedral was Dushma's favourite place. In her daydreams she imagined herself growing up and going to work there, maybe as a caretaker or a guide. She could spend hours just watching the coloured light from the stained-glass windows creeping over the floor. Or she would wander round the nave, peering up at the saints and gargoyles tucked away in their alcoves. Some were carved from granite, while others were cast in copper or bronze and set with semi-precious stones. Their glittering eyes made her wonder what it might be like to be a statue in a niche in the wall. Things would look different, she supposed, more like how they might appear to a tree, if it could see. Which events registered and which did not would be governed by a completely different timescale to the one she was used to. The comings and goings of people, for example, would be too fleeting and trivial to be worthy of attention; the only things that would be noticeable would be the wearing down of flagstones and the rise and fall of walls, like the growth of plants in a speeded-up film.

Loitering in the cloisters of the cathedral one wet afternoon — she couldn't afford a ticket to climb a spire — Dushma fell into conversation with a verger. From him she first learned the lurid story of London's last Catholic martyr, with whose feast-day her birthday coincided. She would later hear or read several other versions, but the outline of the narrative was always broadly the same.

St Gotha had been indicted for practising witchcraft and advocating various heresies such as universal suffrage, evolution and the heliocentric solar system. Even at the time her arrest and trial were widely held to have been a fit-up planned by reactionary industrialists in league with the Church of England. Nevertheless she was found guilty and sentenced to death by burning. Though powerless to save her life, a famous social reformer of the time, Sir Terence Elkie, came forward at the last moment with a much more humane proposal for her execution, far more in tune, he claimed, with the enlightened times in which they lived. And so instead of being burned at a pyre, St Gotha was tied to a ten-metre-high metal pole and left out in a thunderstorm. Sure enough she was struck by lightning, but many eyewitnesses claimed that, after her body had been taken down, it continued to glow with a strange, ethereal light for several days. There was even a detailed written description, from a reliable source, of St Gotha lying in her coffin, a fuzzy white light infusing the air above her. Appropriately, instead of lighting a votive candle in St Gotha's, worshippers bought a tiny light bulb, which they could then screw into one of a long row of sockets below a hologram of the saint in the south transept.

Had Auntie Megan ever shown concern about her absences, Dushma was prepared to use anecdotes like this as evidence that her excursions were educational. But the eventuality never arose. "If a stranger gets you in his car," Auntie Megan once remarked, "you want cash not sweeties, got me, dearie?" And that was all she ever said on the matter.

It was in a concrete sixties multi-storey car park half an hour's walk from the viaduct that Dushma first met Alison Catfinger. A tall, blonde girl about Dushma's age, she was leaning over a parapet on the top floor, watching office workers coming and going in the road below.

She was playing hookey, she said. "Why else would I be 'anging out in a dump like this?"

"It is pretty grim," agreed Dushma, looking round at the stained concrete walls and the oily, tyre-marked floor. She had only ventured in because it was the tallest structure in the vicinity and she had hoped there might be a view. "It's neo-brutalist," she pronounced, wanting to impress the worldly-looking girl.

Alison Catfinger gave a short bark of laughter. "Wasn't 'e in that 'eavy metal band? Didn't know 'e built buildings an' all."

"Who did?"

"Neil Brutalist, of course."

"Oh. No, I meant…"

"Honey," drawled Alison Catfinger, settling her pale, full-bodied figure more comfortably against the parapet, "I may be skipping school but that dun't mean I'm stupid." She looked Dushma up and down, taking in with quiet disdain the drab selection of Auntie Megan's hand-me-downs she wore. "An' I wouldn't be surprised if I knew a sight more 'bout buildings than you do about clothes." Then she smiled with sudden warmth and said, "You can have a go on my skateboard if you like, though."

After that they met there quite often, each unconsciously sensing kinship with a fellow outcast. Dushma liked to outline the hypothetical course of their meteoric rise to lip-synching teen duet pop-stardom. Alison quietly and angrily deplored the dress-sense of every woman who passed beneath their vantage point. ("Look at *her*, oh my *God* what a *squaw*! That jacket came out of a charity shop, I bet you. She needs a *total* makeover.")

In the evenings, after the cars had gone, they trundled round the empty car park on Alison's skateboard. Usually they just went backwards and forwards on the flat. Sometimes they jumped the board off the kerb, or tried to go the other way, flipping the front wheels up on to the pavement. Once, daringly, they went all the way down the spiral up-ramp.

"But what if we meet someone coming the other way?"

"You're frightened, intcha!"

"No, I'm not. Bet *you* are!"

"Rubbish! Done it loads of times."

So then they had to. They did it together, both climbing on to the skateboard at the same time, Alison muttering, "It's a cinch," and "Piece of cake," and other slogans of bravado as she shoved them away from the wall. Then she closed her eyes, clung to Dushma and screamed in terror the whole way down. It was quite exhilarating.

One afternoon Alison carved their names on the car park wall with a penknife. She had to write them both because Dushma wouldn't do her own.

"I mean, I know it's a dump, but it still doesn't seem quite right…"

"Oh, come on, just look at this wall. One more won't make a lot of difference. Nobody's even gunna notice."

"Well, exactly. What's the point?"

While Alison scratched away at the crumbling concrete, Dushma examined the other items of graffiti. "Look at all the other people who've already put their names. Do you know them? Bozo, Scuzz, Samantha … Zeus! Hey look, Zeus has been here! What d'you think he was up to?"

"Always comin' dahn 'ere wunne? Puttin' mortals up the duff!"

"Well *I'd* want more than sweeties if I got into *his* car…"

22

Alison shrieked with laughter.

"…And look at all the names underneath, as well. You can't even make out half of them. Hey, you know what this is, don't you? It's a palimpsest."

"A what?"

"A … a thing that's been written over lots of times."

"Hey. How come you know all these words, if you don't even go to school?"

Dushma shrugged. "Books … the telly. Anyway, I wish I did go to school."

The way Alison described it, school was the most fun anyone could possibly have. It was a world of games lessons, crushes and gang feuds. There were coach rides to swimming pools, termly trips abroad with smuggled alcohol in thermos flasks, and music lessons in a studio. Science classes seemed particularly exciting, sounding in Alison's anecdotes like a cross between fireworks night and urban guerrilla warfare.

"…So I stuck the lighted taper in and it went up like a petrol bomb!" she recounted breathlessly to Dushma. "You could hardly see for the smoke. I was picking bits of test tube out of my hair all afternoon!

"And we play strip poker in between the lessons, did I tell you? Just for a dare. The boys ain't allowed to watch or we get them afterwards. We twist their arms! The secret is, you hang your blouse over the back of your chair, so if you hear the teacher coming you can just like shrug it on dead quick."

But even as she listened enviously to these stories, Dushma couldn't quite suppress the thought that if school was such an interesting place, then why was Alison killing time with her in a gloomy sixties multi-storey car park?

When Alison Catfinger wasn't enjoying herself at school or killing time in the multi-storey car park, she went shoplifting for cosmetics in Boots. She would turn up wearing lurid false nails like talons, her face a bruise of rouge and mascara applied inexpertly but to striking effect. Though envious of her spoils, Dushma never quite dared to accompany her. She didn't feel she could ask Alison to get her something either, as this would make her an accessory before the fact. And as Alison was always telling her, she just didn't know how to accessorize.

"Listen, Dushma lovey, with your complexion you could get away with *anything*. How about a floaty gossamer faux chiffon neckerchief with gold mesh-effect metallic foil interweave and purple silk tasselled fringe, £49.95 from Buyzantium?" She looked slyly sideways at Dushma. "Go on, you *know* you wannit."

"But what if you get caught?"

"What, again you mean? Three strikes an' you're out, innit? Lose your registration. Then it's the workhouse for me. Can't be worse than school anyway."

"But I thought you…"

"Oh, Dush honey, don't be such a *squaw*! School's OK, but not for the whole of your life, you know? See those

24

tribes of office girlies in sensible stockings trudging in and out of work every weekday of their lives? Don't you just know the highlight of their day is a giggle round the drinks machine in their tea break? How can you live when you know the greatest moment of your life was in a spelling test in third-year English?" She folded her arms dramatically and stared away into the distance. As if repeating a line from a song or a film, she said: "There comes a time when you gotta let go, you know?"

"But what about your parents?" persisted Dushma. "What would they say?"

Alison shrugged. "My mum couldn't care less," she said. "And my dad, 'e 'ates me like poison anyway."

"What? Why?"

At first Alison wouldn't say. All her bravado gone, she drew patterns on the concrete floor with her foot and refused to meet Dushma's eye. "Where you from, Welfare?" she asked bitterly. "You'll be askin' me to look at them stupid ink blots next."

"I'm sorry, you're right, it's none of my—"

"If you must know," Alison interrupted, "when I was little they decided I 'ad 'behavioural difficulties'." A sneer in her voice, she went on, "Which seemed to mean I di'n't like sittin' round bein' *bored*, or playin' stupid *games* with child psychologists. So they cut their losses, di'n't they. Why throw good money after bad, they said. They blamed my parents. Wouldn't allow 'em to 'ave more children. But my dad, 'e blamed *me*."

25

"But they can't do that! I mean, stop people having children? Can they?"

"As good as. At least, if you can't afford it all yourself. They won't give you any help with looking after 'em, see?"

Dushma said nothing. She was staring at her friend with her eyes wide.

"I can't b'lieve you don't know all this." Alison shook her head pityingly. "It's the facts of modern life, ain't it? Lucky me gets to go to school and flick paper pellets at Susie Lomax in biology. I get my teeth seen to for free and glasses if my eyes go bad. But if my parents 'ave more children, they've got no choice but to send 'em to sweat to death in the workhouse or leave 'em starving in the gutter. I told my dad 'e should count 'imself lucky that at least 'e's got me. But 'e dun't seem to see it quite like that."

Dushma was still trying to think of a suitable reply when Alison suddenly threw back her head in a gesture of mock defiance. "So you see," she said, her old swagger regained, "I'm on my own, honey."

"Oh, don't say that. Hey, I know what! Listen: in case something happens to you, we'll have to think of a way you can send a message, and then I could … I could…" Dushma trailed off into silence as she realized that she had no idea what on earth she would be able to do.

"That's really sweet of you, Dush," said Alison. "But don't worry, if I get caught again it'll be different. I know the right people now. I've got insurance, you could call it. If the worst comes to the worst, I can get myself off the hook."

"So you're not on your own!" Dushma pressed her. "Come on, who do you know?"

But that was all Alison would say.

That evening in the kitchen, Mr Mackenzie didn't seem interested in talking politics. He wanted to show Dushma how to make a seal out of a bent paper clip and a sliver of cardboard.

"Never mind that now," Dushma persisted. "Is it true they can stop you having children?"

"Well, in a way, I suppose," said Mr Mackenzie reluctantly. "It's a big investment, isn't it. All that education, health care if you get sick. So if it looks like someone might not be able to repay their debt to society, for some reason, then the government won't make the investment in them in the first place. And then you're stuck, unless you can afford to pay for it all yourself."

"They never let me 'ave none." Auntie Megan stood in the kitchen doorway, a half-empty sherry bottle dangling from one hand. "They did some tests. Said I had an 'addictive personality'. Couldn't get car insurance neither – back when I could've afforded a car, that is." She focused her bleary gaze with difficulty on Dushma.

"…And then you put the cardboard here," said Mr Mackenzie. "Like this, to make its flippers."

Like Dushma, Alison hardly ever had any money. Whenever either of them did have any they would go and buy fish and chips or hamburgers. Alison reasoned that fast food was harder to steal than the other sorts of things she wanted. Entirely independently, Dushma reasoned that while they were in a fast food outlet, there was less chance of Alison getting them both into trouble by trying to steal something.

The multi-storey car park they frequented was an irregular source of revenue. Sometimes money fell from people's pockets when they got into or out of their vehicles. And there were four public telephones at the bottom of the stairwell, which Alison habitually checked for abandoned or forgotten change.

Dushma had convinced herself that there was nothing wrong with this. Nevertheless she felt a jolt of apprehension when, during one of their periodic investigations, the phone right next to them began to ring.

By contrast, Alison seemed unperturbed. She stared at the phone for a second or two, then reached out, picked up the receiver and raised it to her ear. She listened in silence for several moments, absently flicking the flap of the reject coin slot with one glossy fingernail. Then she returned the receiver to its cradle.

"Wrong number," she said, turning to Dushma with a shrug.

"Oh."

"Well, what were you expecting?" Alison was scraping one palm over the other as if her hands were sticky.

"I don't know. Someone ... who needed rescuing, maybe."

"I suppose it could've been a pervert. You know what you do then, don't you? You scream as loud as you can!" Alison screwed her eyes shut, stuck her fingers in her ears and let out a prolonged and piercing shriek.

They practised deterring perverts for a while, the concrete stairwell providing a satisfying echo chamber for their efforts. Then they climbed to the top floor of the car park to watch the evening sun.

Sitting with their backs to the wall, they drank Bailey's from a bottle that Alison had stolen from a corner shop. At first Dushma wouldn't touch it.

"Oh, Dushie love, go *on*!" wheedled Alison. "Just a sip. Live a little, hey? Assert your independence. You wouldn't want me to be drinking on my own, would you, they say that's bad, you know. And anyway it's lovely. It tastes like chocolate."

At last Dushma gave in and took a sip. It tasted like chocolate, only not so nice.

Usually when Auntie Megan's lodgers left they did so quietly, often in the night without a word of goodbye. But the departure of the last Mr Mackenzie was utterly different, and Dushma might have been alarmed to witness it, had she not returned home irritable from a headache and with a sickly vapour of Bailey's rising from her churning stomach.

She had stopped to rest at the top of the stairs, the blood pounding in her temples after the long climb up the spiral staircase. When she heard the sound of feet and raised

29

voices, she shrank instinctively into the dark shadow of the metal gate leading on to the landing.

Mr Mackenzie stumbled out of their flat, clutching a suitcase, his overcoat hastily buttoned. His normally placid demeanour had vanished and he turned to stand doggedly hunched but unflinching as Auntie Megan harangued him from the doorway.

"You'd never risk it!" she screamed with shrill contempt. "You wouldn't dare tell anybody anything. And you know they don't even care, they'll just turn a blind eye anyway!"

"Not if I tell 'em, they can't. Official complaint!"

"You wouldn't dare, after all I've done for you!"

"It'd be for her own good! You know she looks on you like a mother… What you're doing isn't just treachery, it's … it's obscene, it's…"

"Oh, don't be so sentimental, she's old enough. And just tell me exactly what else is she supposed to do, eh? I gave my word and I've kept it. It's better than the workhouse. You've gone 'oity-toity, that's your trouble! Think you deserve to hang out with better people than us, eh? Well, you're wrong!"

"You know fine well that's got nothing to do with it. At that age anyone's too young to go on the streets."

"Oh, and just what else do you suggest?" asked Auntie Megan, dropping her voice to a malevolent croon. "She goes on living here like Lady Muck while I wait on her hand and foot for the rest of my life? Not bloomin' likely on the money I was getting from you, you old skinflint!"

30

With the air of a man who has had enough, Mr Mackenzie flung his suitcase to the ground and thrust his head forward, his moustache bristling. But before he could say anything more, Auntie Megan leapt nimbly back into the hallway and slammed the door in his face.

"What difference does it make? She spends most of her time on the streets as it is!" came her taunting voice from inside the flat. "And that's where you can go for all I care, 'cos you're not coming back in 'ere!"

Mr Mackenzie held himself rigid for another moment or two. Then he relaxed, shrugged, picked up his case again and walked to the head of the stairs. When he saw Dushma he jumped. Recovering himself, he smiled at her as if nothing had happened. "Just off," he said casually, hefting his suitcase. "Why don't you come, hmm? We'll go somewhere nice. France maybe. Or Amsterdam. Somewhere on the train."

Dushma shook her head.

"No, of course not. Trains. Tickets. Difficult. Silly of me, ha ha ha." He hesitated, then leaned towards her. His breath went scraping fast in and out of his nostrils. "You watch yourself," he muttered. "She'll sell you, see? She'll sell you for a bottle of gin."

Then he clattered hurriedly down the iron stairs, his bobbing shadow thrown in front of him by the light of the naked bulb dangling high above the landing.

Dushma let herself quietly into the flat and went through into the kitchen. Auntie Megan stood at the sink, head thrown back and a bottle held to her lips. She was dressed to go out, in high heels, wide-meshed tights and a sequinned frock.

She spun round when she heard Dushma enter. The bottle-top dropped from her fingers and bounced spinning up from the tiles.

"Haven't you got anything better to do?" she snapped. "Creeping around, spying on people. Can't you do something useful?"

"Like what?" asked Dushma, equally eager for a fight. "Get dolled up and go out on the town?"

"Ungrateful bitch!" screamed Auntie Megan. "I've never had a penny for you from the social! Everything you've ever had from me I've had to earn it! And is this gratitude? You're as bad as your mother. Like you're living on some other planet! I told her not to have you but she thought she knew better. And now it's not her who's lived to regret it, it's me. Too kind for my own good, that's my trouble."

"Oh, I'm so sorry to be such a nuisance to you. I know you tried your best to make sure I wouldn't be!"

"How *dare* you! You don't know what you're talking about!"

"...And now aren't I *awful*, squandering all these *wonderful* opportunities you've given me. I'm sure I wouldn't have turned out such a wastrel if only I'd had the benefit of your education. Or any education at all, actually."

"Hark at her. Taught you to count din' I? And all about

the birds and the bees. And that's all you're going to need, believe me."

"Oh I see, so is that all I'm supposed to know? A-B-C, 1-2-3. Might as well close down all the senior schools then, mightn't they?"

"Self-sufficiency, that's what I've taught you, even if you're too stupid to realize it yet. Well, don't worry, because you'll soon get the chance to learn everything I know. And if you've got any sense you'll be very grateful for a little professional knowledge when the time comes. You can do it the hard way or you can do it the easy way, but in the end you ain't going to have no choice."

Auntie Megan smirked suggestively as she said this, and Dushma was reminded uncomfortably of Mr Mackenzie's warning. "It's not like you ever *tried* to give me a choice, is it?" she spat. "Kept here like a … a slave, or a wanted criminal, not allowed to have a proper life, just so you don't get into trouble. What right have you got to deprive me of the advantages everyone else gets, just to make sure they don't find out about *you*? How dare you talk about selfishness?"

"Oh, so it's my fault now is it?" Auntie Megan had lowered her voice to a poisonous whisper. "Well, if you really want to know … I suppose you'll just have to be told."

"Told? Told what?" asked Dushma, suddenly apprehensive.

Auntie Megan said nothing, merely pushing her way past

Dushma and out of the kitchen. A look of determination on her face, she crossed the hallway and went into her bedroom, high heels clattering on the floorboards.

Dushma stood in the kitchen doorway, torn between curiosity and a reluctance to let Auntie Megan have the satisfaction of the last word. As she hesitated, Auntie Megan emerged from her bedroom, a tight smile of triumph on her lips, and thrust an A4-sized piece of smoky celluloid into Dushma's hands.

"There," said Auntie Megan triumphantly. "So now you know. And about time too. Can't think why I didn't show you before."

"But ... what is it? What does it mean?"

"What does it *mean*, she asks. Well, why don't you just go and ask a specialist? If you dare! They said you might be ill. Or dangerous. They wanted to do some tests. They were *very* interested. That was when your mother got too scared to go back to the hospital."

Dushma stared uncomprehendingly at the shiny surface of the photograph she held. She still couldn't tell what it was supposed to be.

"So *next* time you're tempted to start giving yourself airs," mocked Auntie Megan, "just be grateful for what you get from me, because it's more than you'll get from anybody else!"

She hitched her minuscule PVC handbag up on to her shoulder and stalked out of the flat, slamming the door behind her.

Dushma went into the kitchen and held the rectangle of celluloid up to the light of the bare bulb. Now it was possible to tell that the photograph showed an image like an X-ray of the inside of a pregnant woman. She could make out the whitish segments of the mother's vertebrae and the crouching shape of the foetus inside her distended stomach. The picture was mostly black and white, except in the region of the unborn baby's head. Here the celluloid was stained with vivid pools of light. The colours reminded Dushma of the patches of orange and purple that swam behind her eyelids when she closed her eyes after looking too long at a bright light.

Still none the wiser, she scanned the photograph again. Even on closer inspection, there were no clues as to why Auntie Megan should consider it such damning proof of Dushma's second-class status.

There was some writing in one corner, but it was mostly too faded to be legible. All that could be made out were some initials: EEG, they read. Well, *they* weren't her initials. The photograph must be of somebody else. There had been a mistake. It was someone called ... Evelyn, perhaps. Evelyn Elizabeth Grant. Dushma could picture her already. The child of rich parents, living in an enormous house with a garden and attending a private school with science labs and an orchestra. Perhaps she herself was really Evelyn Grant, swapped at birth! In a film she would be identified by a faithful old retainer who recognized her from a tell-tale birthmark. Did she have a tell-tale birthmark? She would look, next time she was in the bath. Depending where it was, it might take some ingenious plotting to have the old retainer discover it innocently.

Her daydream evaporated abruptly and her resentment returned with redoubled strength. *Ill*, Auntie Megan had said. *Or dangerous*. But apart from coughs and colds she had never felt ill in her life. And the thought of anyone regarding her as dangerous was absurd.

This photograph didn't prove anything. It could be anybody. She should have ripped the thing in half and flung it back into Auntie Megan's face. "I don't care what it means!" she should have said. "It doesn't mean you're not a miserable, tight-fisted, cruel old shrew!"

She was tempted to tear it up anyway and leave the remains on Auntie Megan's dressing table. Instead she decided to keep it, just in case it could be used as evidence of her mistaken identity. She hid it under her bed until she could think of somewhere safer to put it.

Then she took her revenge by gathering all the bottles of sherry and spirits she could find and tipping their contents into the kitchen sink. Still spluttering from the alcoholic vapours rising from the plughole, she left the empty bottles lying blatantly on the draining board and locked herself in her room.

IV

Dushma slept late the following morning and when she woke her throat was sore and her tongue was stuck to the roof of her mouth. She dressed quietly and then left her room, a little apprehensive about meeting Auntie Megan. She was tempted to go out straight away and be sure of avoiding her altogether, except she was desperate for a drink of water.

In fact she had the flat to herself. There was no sign of Auntie Megan. Kitchen and living room were empty, and the sunlight streamed in through the window of the main bedroom and across an unruffled counterpane.

Dushma stood by the bed and curled the toes of her stocking feet around the pile of a fake fur rug on the floor. She looked around for any sign of where her aunt might be, but everything was as usual. The room had its habitual air, spartan yet cluttered, like an untidy hotel room. The wardrobe door was ajar, revealing ranks of dresses and shoes. Hairbrushes, make-up and some cheap paste jewellery lay scattered on the dressing table. Some dusty hatboxes lined a shelf above the window. These were almost all the things Auntie Megan owned.

A buzzer sounded in the hallway. Dushma jumped, then went slowly out to the intercom on the wall. Auntie Megan must have forgotten her keys. How dreary. Perhaps she had rung the buzzer before but Dushma hadn't heard it in her sleep. She wouldn't be happy, and Dushma didn't feel she could muster the energy for a row. She also found herself feeling a little guilty, as if caught in a forbidden act. What had she been thinking in Auntie Megan's bedroom? She suddenly wondered whether, left alone a little longer, she would have begun to go through her aunt's belongings.

The buzzer sounded again. "Hello yes," said Dushma wearily.

"Good morning. Is that Miss Megan Crate?"

"Oh. No … no, I'm sorry, I…"

"This is Detective Inspector Rapplemann. If you're not too busy my colleagues and I would rather like to come up for a chat."

Dushma didn't answer. Her mind had gone blank. She stared straight ahead at her forefinger, rigid against the button of the intercom, and concentrated on the white half-moon of bloodless flesh beneath her nail.

"I must warn you that, should you choose not to cooperate, we are empowered to effect an entry by whatever means necessary in order to carry out a search of the premises."

Dushma shook herself and pulled her hand away from the intercom, cutting off the hiss of static and the boom of traffic from the street far below. The silence rang in her ears. She pivoted this way and that, her palm pressed to her mouth.

This was the moment she had been warned of, time and again for as long as she could remember. She was going to be taken away, sent somewhere awful and punished for not having let herself be taken away before.

She forced herself to be calm and to think through the possibilities. Perhaps something had happened to Auntie Megan and they had come to tell her. But what had they said? *Effect an entry ... search the premises*. Search for what? Surely they would see soon enough that there was nothing to hide? And then... But no, ridiculous. Even if they weren't looking for her, at some point they would ask to see her registration card: they'd want a name, a number, some form of official ID, even from the patently innocent such as herself. And then, when she couldn't produce what they wanted, she would be discovered.

She ran to the front door, eased it open and tiptoed across the landing, trying not to disturb the rickety planks. It occurred to her that this was pointless, even as she did it, because of course they knew exactly where she was.

She peered down over the banisters. Already she thought she could hear the clang of boots far down the wrought-iron steps.

Back in the flat she locked the door and looked for things

to barricade it with, but found nothing. On a nail beside the intercom hung the heavy iron key to the gate at the top of the spiral staircase. Should she lock that as well? Did she have time to go out on to the landing again? Would it make any difference in the end? The only way she was going to escape was if they couldn't find her.

There was nothing to hide in their flat, and nowhere to hide it either. The only cupboard big enough for Dushma to fit into was Auntie Megan's wardrobe: a childish, birthday party hiding place for when hiding is more scary than being caught.

Which left the railway. She exhaled a humourless breath of laughter: climb up through the trapdoor on the landing and leap on a passing train like a cowboy outlaw in a western, leaving the posse perplexed in the settling dust. She grimaced in despairing self-mockery, shook her head and rubbed her hands over her face.

Detective Inspector Rapplemann forced the door himself. He didn't have to do that kind of thing; there were two strong constables behind him. But he liked the weight of the crowbar in his hands, the springy feel of the jamb as it shattered with a slow crackle into a sappy-smelling spray of splintery quills.

The broken door creaked slowly inwards. Flakes of paint pattered to the floor. The three policemen stepped into the hall.

"Search the place," instructed Rapplemann, hooking the

curled end of the crowbar over his forearm. "And if you find any padlocked boxes or cupboards – just leave them to me."

The two constables went from room to room, their heavy boots booming or swishing according to whether they trod on bare floorboards or Auntie Megan's rugs. They rifled wardrobes and tapped walls. They peered under beds and looked on top of cupboards. But despite their thoroughness, it took them only minutes to ascertain that there was no one in the flat.

"Are you sure?" snapped Rapplemann, standing with his arms folded in the middle of the living room.

"Yes, sir. Positive," said one of the constables. "Couldn't hide a cat in this dump, sir."

Rapplemann turned abruptly away and began to pace back and forth. An instinct had told him that his tip-off was genuine and now he felt made a fool of, but when he spoke no one would have been able to guess his anger.

"You think so, Constable?" he asked in a conversational tone. He put one hand to his chin and looked appraisingly round the room. "A dump, you say? Oh, I don't know, loft living's becoming quite fashionable, apparently. South-facing, gets the sunlight. A very commanding aspect. You could do quite a lot with this place, if you had a little imagination. Terracotta tiling on the floor, an Impressionist print or two … I find Degas looks so *right* on bare brick walls, don't you? Picture it: a few Philippe Starck light-fittings, modern flat-pack furniture, unglazed ceramic ornaments…" He spun abruptly on his heel. "So! Now that our imaginations have had a little exercise, let's put them to work, shall we, and ask ourselves: a panic-stricken fugitive, a parasite on society fleeing justice – where might she try and hide … in a dump like this?"

Dushma often watched the television in Auntie Megan's kitchen. Perhaps because of their proximity to the electrified railway lines, the only way they could get a decent signal for their old black and white portable was by putting it on top of a high cupboard. So when people said that too much TV was bad for you, Dushma knew that this was true: it gave you a crick in the neck.

The ache she was feeling now in between her shoulder blades was a little similar to the one she got when she'd been standing in the kitchen for too long looking up at the television. But the pain in her arms was much, much worse. This must be what it felt like to be torn apart by wild horses.

Her feet were dangling in space, already going numb. She could feel them buzzing. Looking down, she could see the mesmerizing turn of the giant fan in the underground railway ventilation shaft. It seemed deceptively close, as if she could just step down on to it.

She was hanging from the metal bars of the grille outside the near-horizontal living-room window. She could hear the voices and footsteps of Detective Inspector Rapplemann and the two constables, and was praying that one of them wouldn't think to clamber up the curving far wall of the living room, look down through the window, and see her clenched white knuckles and gently swaying body.

The tendons stretching from her armpits to each elbow felt like over-inflated balloons about to explode. She cast her thoughts about wildly to try and distract herself from the agony. A for Adolescence in the *Encyclopaedia Britannica*. She'd read that your arms and legs grew faster than the rest of you. That's why teenagers were best at swimming. She couldn't have done this if she'd been older. Mr Mackenzie ... he'd said he used to squeeze tennis balls. She now felt thankful for all the times she'd trudged up the spiral iron staircase, two carrier bags full of Auntie Megan's shopping clinking in each hand.

The fan swirled round and round beneath her feet. Her ribs were like harps in her chest. Wouldn't it be easier just to let go and drop, her hair and clothes billowing around her, and let the rising column of air from the ventilation shaft catch her and waft her gently down like Mr Mackenzie's parachute?

She couldn't hear the voices any more. Perhaps they'd gone. Or perhaps it was a trap and they were waiting for her? No, she told herself fiercely, they'd *prefer* it if she fell; it would make things easier for them. It would be less messy. Suddenly she wanted to giggle. Well, maybe the paperwork anyway.

She must pull herself together. She was getting hysterical. The blood was pulsing in her muscles, her forearms were trembling and she felt that she was about to lose control of her hands. She couldn't afford to wait any longer. She heaved herself upwards and crooked her arms round one of the metal bars.

She had managed to lower the window shut after herself on her way out and now her head banged sharply against the glass above her. She sucked in a deep gasp of air and held her breath, waiting for discovery. Nothing happened. She breathed out with a ragged sob. Pushing up with one elbow, she threw the window inwards on its hinges. It swung open with a crash. Still nothing happened.

She pulled and dragged herself awkwardly up through the narrow gap between the bars and over the sill, banging and scraping her knees and elbows as she sought whatever purchase she could. Released from tension, her arms blazed hot and cold and jerked unpredictably when she tried to move them.

She lay limp for a few minutes to try and recover her strength. Then she sat up, slid down the curved wall to the floor of the living room and stood up carefully. One of the panes had broken when she flung the window open and there were slivers of glass here and there.

Staggering a little as the circulation in her feet slowly returned to normal, she went as quickly and quietly as she could into her bedroom. The door of her wardrobe yawned drunkenly open, one hinge torn away. Her clothes had been thrown all over the floor in the policemen's hurried search.

She retrieved her leather satchel from where it had been

flung into a corner and began to gather up those of her few possessions she intended to take with her. From the jumble of articles around her she picked out a bottle of bath crystals from The Body Shop, a penknife with two blades and a pair of tweezers, a hairbrush with a carved wooden handle, her postcard of the hologram of St Gotha from the cathedral and a small pile of money she had hidden at the back of a drawer in case of emergencies. Seeing a corner of celluloid sticking out from under the bed, she also took the photograph Auntie Megan had given her the night before.

Turning to her scattered collection of clothes, she hastily selected a change of underwear, her favourite blouse and skirt combination, and a satin scarf the colour of autumn leaves that Alison Catfinger had stolen and pressed upon her despite her admittedly feeble protests. She ignored the lurid lycra micro-skirts and see-through black nylon tops that Auntie Megan had recently taken to buying for her.

She quickly scanned her disordered shelves and pulled out a couple of her favourite books, including *Lives and Legends of Historic London*, which had some good maps in it. She hesitated briefly over her guitar, and then decided to leave it. It was light enough, but bulky; carrying it would make her more conspicuous, she thought.

Passing Auntie Megan's room on her way to the front door she noticed a gleam in the sunlight from an item of jewellery that had been swept off the dressing table. It was a gold and silver hairslide studded with coloured glass beads and Dushma had always wanted it. She hesitated for an instant, then darted in, picked it up and thrust it defiantly into her thick, unruly hair. On an impulse, as she left the flat, she also took the heavy iron key to the gate at the top of the spiral staircase.

She hurried across the landing, the floorboards rattling. Then halfway across she froze. *What if they were waiting for her on the stairs?*

As she hesitated, a tiny noise nearby made her turn her head. She was standing opposite the entrance to the derelict flat next door to her own. At first it seemed untouched, but as she looked more closely she noticed fresh scratches in the wood of the jamb next to the lock. Then she heard the noise again: a faint squeak like a rusty bicycle, or...

Almost imperceptibly, the handle was turning.

Before she could move the door to the empty flat flew open. A thin smile of triumph on his lips, Detective Inspector Rapplemann stood poised on the threshold. He lunged towards her, and would have seized her with ease, but the crowbar he still carried cracked against his kneecap and he stumbled.

Dushma lurched away from him and ran towards the stairs. In the time it took the constables to step around the prostrate Rapplemann, she had reached the metal gate at the top and slammed it shut behind her. The key trembled in her hand, rattling against the keyhole as she tried to push it home. The lock snapped shut an instant before the first policeman threw himself against the bars of the gate.

Dushma shrank back and held up the key as if to ward

him off, although the gate held firm. She still nursed a faint hope that this was all a mistake and she could somehow put it right.

"Why don't you just leave me alone?" In her breathlessness it came out sounding all wrong, a sullen mutter instead of a strident cry of innocence. "I haven't done anything. I haven't! What business is it of yours?"

"Now be sensible, young lady," said one of the constables in the reassuring voice he'd been trained to use in such situations. "This isn't going to do you any good at all. So I suggest you just—"

"Stand aside!" snarled Rapplemann, back on his feet, the crowbar swinging high above his head.

He brought it down with a crash against the gate. There was a screech and a flicker of sparks as the forked, flattened end slid down the overlap between the gate and its frame, trying to find its way into the gap.

Dushma leapt backwards in fright, spinning round in the air as she went. Somehow keeping her balance, she hurled herself three at a time down the stairs, holding on to the central column to stop herself banging into the outer wall.

The crashing sounds receded behind her and soon the only noise that accompanied her descent was the thrum of her shoes on the wrought-iron steps. She slowed down, afraid her trembling knees would give and spill her in a heap. The palm of her left hand was burned red and strips of skin were peeling away.

She thought of the three trapped policemen. There was no telephone in the flat, so they couldn't call for help, and they were probably too high up to catch anyone's attention by shouting from a window. What if they starved to death? She could be tried for … well, not murder, because she hadn't meant it, but manslaughter at least.

But somehow she couldn't see Inspector Rapplemann starving to death in Auntie Megan's spartan living room, or even sitting quietly waiting to be rescued.

At the bottom of the stairs was an old wooden door, concealed from the outside by an abandoned plastic wheelie-bin. Pulling it open cautiously, Dushma looked quickly around her and then darted out into the narrow cobbled alleyway. To her left was the buttressed brick leg of the viaduct. Behind the high clapboard hoardings to her right, she could hear the steady churn and rumble of the underground railway extractor fan.

There was a phone box on the corner where the alley opened on to the main street. Perhaps she should tell someone about the policemen in the flat? She could disguise her voice, put on an accent… But no, of course! They must have a radio… They had probably already called for help, given her description to their colleagues in the area…

She turned into the main street. Inspector Rapplemann was kneeling on the pavement less than a stone's throw away from her. Beside him, on its side, lay the life raft from the top of the viaduct, the life raft meant for train-crash victims stranded on the railway track. Nearby were the two constables: one sat on the kerb, cradling his arm; the other lay motionless in the gutter.

Rapplemann saw Dushma immediately. "There she is!" he shouted, pointing. "Stop that girl! Don't let her get away!"

He lurched to his feet and limped towards her, but the crowd around the life raft was already thickening. Recovering from her surprise, Dushma began to hurry in the opposite direction as quickly as she could, slithering nimbly through the gaps between the curious pedestrians. Glancing back, she saw that Rapplemann was already obscured by a knot of passers-by. "Stand aside!" she heard him yell.

Hurrying on, she overheard snatches of conversation from the people she passed.

"What's happening?"

"I don't know, they just landed…"

"Who did? Who's landed?"

"You hear that? They've landed!"

"There's been a train crash!"

"No!"

"Oh yes there has – on the viaduct!"

"What, just here? Is it safe?"

"Hear that? The viaduct's collapsing!"

Dushma zigzagged to the edge of the milling throng gathering round the life raft. She ducked into a narrow passage between two shops, turned again through an arch and down a long, winding flight of steps and then out on to another main street. No one had followed her.

She drifted inconspicuously into the flow of early lunch-time shoppers. She knew these streets as well as her bedroom ceiling, but now she knew she couldn't go back home again she felt like she was seeing them for the first time. Glancing up, she noticed protruding gables and odd clusters of chimneys that she'd never paid attention to before. The sunlight was unusually bright, darting off door handles and windowpanes, showing up interesting alcoves and tunnels and fire escapes. She passed a hot-dog seller's stand and the smell of frying onions seemed particularly vivid.

She should have been worried by her situation but suddenly she wasn't any more. Mr Mackenzie had been right. This was where she felt at home. There was so much to see.

She was going to go to the multi-storey car park to look for Alison Catfinger. Alison would know what to do. She began to think of how she could recount her escapade. "You know you said there comes a time when you've just got to let everything go?" she could say. "Well, guess what…"

Up ahead of her, bobbing above the crowd, she saw a policeman's helmet. She told herself to stay calm. Of course she was going to pass policemen in the street. It didn't mean anything. But she snatched a quick look back over her shoulder nonetheless. A second policeman's helmet was approaching from behind. Its wearer must have been about a hundred metres away but was moving quickly.

Dushma stopped dead in her tracks and let her shoulders

sag. For a moment she was ready to admit defeat, to stand there and wait for them to catch her. It could be worse. At least she hadn't stolen anything – except, she supposed, Auntie Megan's hairslide. And then there was the scarf that Alison…

A shop, she could hide in a shop. A shop with a way out at the back. She looked around her. There was a Marks and Spencer on the opposite side of the road, but crossing over would be too conspicuous. And on this side there was only an underground station.

Dushma had never been in an underground station. She had no idea what to do. Travelling by tube was supposed to be too risky for people who weren't registered.

She took a firm grip on the coins in her pocket, threw back her shoulders and strode into the ticket hall.

V

Although she was squashed so tightly she could hardly breathe, Dushma was enjoying the swaying, rattling motion of the train.

She was clinging with one hand to a strap that hung from the ceiling. Peering out from under her arm, she could see a section of window and, through it, the brick wall of the tunnel flashing by. Attached to the wall was a bunch of coloured wires which, being not quite straight, appeared to wiggle up and down as the train went past. Every now and then the wall vanished, to be replaced by a depthless black abyss in which distant lights or train windows sometimes shone.

When she tired of watching the wall of the tunnel, Dushma twisted herself round to try and get a better look at her fellow passengers. She hadn't expected people on the tube to be any different from those she encountered on the streets, and indeed at first glance she appeared to be in the company of a perfectly ordinary cross-section of society.

But there was a curious, prickly atmosphere, as if she had come upon the aftermath of a bitter row that might be rekindled at any moment by a careless word.

No one was talking, or even looking at anyone else. Despite the overcrowding in the carriage, most of the passengers managed to be reading a book or a newspaper, even though in some cases they had so little space that the print must have been uncomfortably close to their eyes.

One of the men standing nearest to her, letting go of his strap so he could turn a page, lurched sideways and trod on her toe. Instead of apologizing he merely glanced at her in annoyance, tutted under his breath and returned to his reading.

Dushma angled her head to try and see the cartoon strip on the back page of his paper. Noticing what she was doing, he lowered his paper again and glared at her with the look of someone who has been pushed beyond endurance.

"Are you sure you can see all right from there?" he asked sarcastically. "Or would you like me to read it out for you?" Without waiting for her to reply he began to declaim the front-page headlines in a loud and patronizing voice. "'Prince Alfred Opens Sculpture Park in Rotherhithe: Thousands Attend … Weapons Snatched from Historic Armoury: Detectives Baffled by Daring and Mysterious Raid on Priceless McCulloch Collection … Astronomers Forecast Record Sunspot Activity: Season of Summer Storms Predicted…'" Or is that too serious for you? How about your horoscope? What sign are you? Or the problem page: need some advice on your relationship? Or some hints on etiquette…? No, really, it's no trouble, I insist…"

"No, no, it's all right, thank you," muttered Dushma. She had obviously committed a terrible underground *faux pas*. She twisted away, her cheeks hot.

She found herself looking down into the eyes of a tanned, thin-faced man with greying hair. She was standing right in front of his seat and one of his bony knees was digging into her leg. He too had lowered his newspaper and was glaring at her, his eyebrows bunched into a frown. This time she decided that she wouldn't be cowed. She looked back at him defiantly and tilted up her chin a little.

"What are you staring at?" he snapped. He was very well dressed; there was a cashmere scarf draped over his shoulders and a thickly knotted shiny blue tie snuggled complacently between the floppy lapels of his coat.

"I suppose you want me to let you sit down," he went on belligerently. "Just because you're a girl or something. Well, I won't. Unless you're pregnant … maybe. Well? Are you pregnant?"

"You're disgusting," said a man sitting next to him.

"You keep out of this. It's a private conversation."

"No it's not a conversation. *She* hasn't even said anything yet."

"*He* wouldn't give his seat up for the queen, just look at him," said a middle-aged woman, waving dismissively at the well-dressed man.

He ignored her. "Actually, she probably doesn't even

speak English," he confided loudly to the man next to him, looking disdainfully at Dushma's dark-complexioned face.

"Then why bother talking to me in the first place?" demanded Dushma furiously.

"Come to think of it, I really don't know," replied the well-dressed man with a triumphant smirk, returning to his newspaper.

By this time another argument was in progress further down the carriage. "And why should he give up his seat, just because someone's a woman? I wouldn't give my seat up for you!"

"Well if you must know I'd rather collapse from exhaustion than sit in your seat, thank you very much."

At the next stop Dushma pushed her way to the doors. They may have looked normal, but they really were a very cross section of society and she wasn't going to put up with their bickering any more than she had to.

The man who had trodden on her toe earlier elbowed her in the ribs as she squeezed past him.

The adjacent carriage, in contrast to the angry orange of the one she'd just left, was decorated in a cool, relaxing blue. It was much less crowded, too, and she quickly found a seat. She had just settled herself comfortably, her satchel on her knees, when to her horror the well-dressed man from the other carriage sat down next to her. Not wanting to provoke him into making any more sarcastic comments, she turned quickly away from him and tried to absorb herself in the adverts above the windows opposite.

"Ah, I see you like a contrast too," she heard him say pleasantly. Glancing quickly sideways, she saw that he had folded up his newspaper. It lay on his lap along with his ticket, which she noticed was divided diagonally into two colours, orange and blue. "Despite the saying, I've found that unless one makes a conscious effort, what travel tends to do is to *numb* the mind, don't you think?"

Dushma looked at him more carefully. He didn't look like he was waiting for the chance to make fun of her again. Rather, he seemed genuinely interested in her response.

"I don't really know," she said. "...But I heard someone in the ticket hall who couldn't decide whether she wanted sour feeling, or no feeling."

"Let me see ... sour feeling or... Oh, very good! That'll be South Ealing or North Ealing, of course. Ha ha! But one might have thought she wanted some sort of anaesthetic, eh? Now myself," he added, "I've just got back from holiday. But you soon get back in the old routine."

That must be how he had got his tan, thought Dushma. Curiosity got the better of her. "Where did you go?" she asked.

"The Seychelles, actually. I was lucky you see: I fly on business sometimes and I'd saved up some Air Miles."

"I haven't been on holiday for ages," offered Dushma cautiously.

"Well of course, you could always say that living in this great city of ours as we do, with so much on our doorsteps, there's almost no need to go abroad at all. We've got

56

everything, pretty much. The architecture, galleries, the theatre, the shops... I must say that scarf really suits you, by the way... Not always the weather though, alas!"

"Yes, I walk around a lot," said Dushma, charmed in spite of herself. "I think I've probably been in all the churches near the centre. The main ones, anyway."

"Do you visit the museums, too? Extraordinary news about the McCulloch Collection, isn't it?" He pointed at the headline on the front page of the newspaper in his lap. "They say it was a gang of unregistered youths, probably escaped from a workhouse. This crackdown they're promising can't come a moment too soon, if you ask me. I don't see why the rest of us should suffer just because certain people are unable or unwilling to contribute their fair share to society."

For an instant Dushma thought he must suspect her and her mouth went dry. She swallowed. "Absolutely," she said, with what she hoped sounded like conviction, and to her relief the well-dressed man soon changed the subject.

They chatted amiably about buildings and books until the train pulled into the next station. Unfortunately this was his stop, said the well-dressed man. He shook her hand and declared himself delighted to have met her. Then he rose and made his way to the door, smiling and nodding at several other passengers as he went.

Before they reached the next stop an inspector asked to see Dushma's ticket. She hadn't seen him enter the carriage, and didn't realize he was an inspector until he stood in front of her and showed her his badge.

She offered him her bright orange slip of cardboard but he shook his head. "This is polite," he said. "You can't sit in 'ere with an impolite ticket. I'm afraid you're going to have to leave the train. Come along with you. Up. Out. No arguing."

Of course: the blue and orange tickets, the different colour schemes in the carriages. Dushma groaned inwardly at her stupidity. And she'd been so pleased with herself for working out the underground so quickly.

"All right, all right," she muttered, getting to her feet. "What do you say when you throw people out of impolite?"

The train reached the next stop and the doors slid open. An old man in a flat cap and a long dirty raincoat was sitting cross-legged on the platform almost directly in front of her. He was wheezing disconsolately into a mouth organ, and there was a cardboard box in front of him to collect people's change. *She* could have done that, thought Dushma, if only she'd brought her guitar. She wasn't very good, but she'd have been better than the mouth-organ player.

She stepped from the carriage. Trying to save face, she remarked haughtily over her shoulder, "I was getting out here anyway, actually."

But the ticket inspector wasn't finished with her yet. He stepped down behind her and gripped her firmly by the elbow. With his other hand he pulled a walkie-talkie from his belt.

"'Ello 'Arry... Yeah, got another imp tryin' to travel in

polite. What's that? …Yeah, sure, coming right up!" He thumbed the walkie-talkie off and pulled Dushma round to face him, smiling nastily. "Looks like you're going to have to learn some manners 'fore you can travel in polite, my sweetheart. Right then, got your registration card?"

"No," said Dushma, her shoulders slumped. She couldn't be bothered to try the pantomime of beginning to search her satchel. She felt sure that what had worked at the ticket window wouldn't be enough to satisfy the inspector.

"Eh? What d'yer mean, you forgotten it?"

"No," said Dushma dully. Other passengers were hurrying by, glancing quickly at Dushma as they passed and then looking away. But the old man with the mouth organ had stopped playing and was staring at her intently.

"You mean you're not…Wait a minute… 'Ere 'Arry, 'Arry! She ain't registered… What? …We can what? Yeah, right! …*How* much? Jesus!"

The old man had gathered up his cardboard box of change and risen to his feet. He was now sidling off down the platform, looking backwards as he went and jerking his head significantly. Then he turned abruptly off to one side beneath a sign that said EMERGENCY EXIT.

The inspector's grip had slackened on her arm. "What d'yer mean, fifty-fifty? 'Old on a sec, who found 'er, eh? Was it me or was it… But I don't need to lock 'er in your sodding locker… You've got what? …You've got some string? But 'Arry, she ain't strugglin', she's as…"

Dushma pulled her elbow free and spun round so that

her satchel swung into the inspector's stomach. Then she threw herself along the platform after the old man with the mouth organ. Behind her, passengers glanced quickly at the panting, bent-double ticket inspector, then looked away and hurried on.

VI

The old man moved very quickly for someone who had looked so decrepit. Since she had ducked after him into the narrow tunnel hidden behind a fire hose, Dushma had hardly been able to keep up.

The light was dim and often all she could see of him was a faint shadow in front of her. Now and then he paused and she heard him counting under his breath – "First left, second left, *third* left" – before darting off down a side tunnel. She began to worry she would lose sight of him altogether, particularly when the roof became so low that they were both forced to drop to their hands and knees.

Dushma's legs were beginning to feel like soggy cardboard underneath her. When at last they emerged from the low section of tunnel she found that she couldn't get to her feet again.

"Stop! Wait a minute … I can't … I've got, got to stop." She slumped sideways and pulled herself up into a sitting position, the curved tunnel wall at her back.

61

She couldn't remember the old man turning round and retracing his steps. The next thing she knew, a blinding torchlight was shining in her eyes and an insistent voice was questioning her.

"Which cell are you from? How did you get here? How many of you are there? Come on, God damn it, answer me! Then at least if I have to leave you it won't have all been for nothing."

"I don't know," mumbled Dushma sleepily. "I haven't come from anywhere. I live … I used to live in the viaduct. There was only one of me … and Alison, sometimes, in the car park."

"Don't think I'm so stupid. They'd've caught you years ago. Now stop wasting time and tell me who you are. Who sent you? What were your instructions? Are you carrying a message? What do you want? How did you find out about us?"

"I *told* you," snapped Dushma, annoyance restoring her strength a little. "Nobody's sent me from anywhere, and I couldn't care less who you are!"

With a groan the old man lowered his torch and turned away from her. He pulled off his hat and dashed it to the ground in exasperation. A cloud of dust swirled round his head. Dushma caught the smell of talcum powder. That must be what made his hair seem grey. And now she looked more closely, the lines on his face seemed artificial too.

The old man wasn't an old man at all, but a thin, jug-eared boy who couldn't have been more than about fifteen, even though with his heavy, bunched jaw and deep-set, squinting eyes he had been able to pass for much older.

"Brilliant," he said sarcastically, talking more to himself than to her. "Frogging brilliant. Might've blown our cover 'cos of you, and now you don't know anything. I'll tell you what an' all: Ibmahuj is going to kill me."

"What's that? Who's going to kill you? Why, what've you done?"

"*She* couldn't care less who *we* are. What earthly use is *she* going to be, eh?" There was a rattle of change as the boy began to go through his pockets. "Missed the lunch-time rush because of you. Fifty pence, that's all I got. Fifty frogging pee!"

"Oh, shut up for heaven's sake! If you must know, I think you were lucky to get that much, the noises you were making."

The boy looked up at the ceiling. "I save her from the workhouse and now I have to put up with this? I ask you!"

Dushma pulled herself to her feet. "OK. All right. Fine. Don't worry, I'll just go back if you'd rather." The boy merely shrugged. Reaching into an inside pocket of his coat, he pulled out a pair of headphones and settled them dismissively over his ears before turning round and walking away.

After a few seconds Dushma hurried on after him.

The tunnels began to get wider. Some parts of the floor were inlaid with sleepers, although there were no rails.

63

There were almost no lights now and the boy was going more slowly, picking his way by the light of the torch.

"Where are we going?" Dushma wanted to know, catching up with him as he paused. "Is it much further? I may have to rest."

They were standing at a T-junction leading into a much larger tunnel. Instead of replying, the boy peered cautiously round the brick arch of the debouchment and shone his torch first one way, then the other. He had pulled his headphones down around his neck and a faint sound like rustling foil could just be heard from the earpieces.

"After you," he said, pointing with his torch in the direction she should take.

Trying to seem nonchalant, Dushma stepped around the corner.

Something loomed up in front of her, appearing to move in the wavering torchlight as its shadow danced on the wall behind it. She caught a glimpse of dully shining teeth and spread, skeletal wings.

The entire width of the tunnel seemed filled by a giant metal bat.

She jerked backwards, unable to stifle a scream. Spinning round to run, she saw the boy grinning maliciously at her. Turning back to look again, she saw that the creature was inert.

It lay on the floor of the tunnel like a burned-out aeroplane on the runway. A fierce heat had blackened the metal skeleton of its wings and scorched the wooden sleepers underneath it. Dangling strands of some charred outer covering still adhered to its wire framework, trembling in a gentle draught. Through the exposed ribs of the body its insides were visible, a melted mess of cog wheels and blistered printed circuit boards. The head lay twisted sideways, mouth gaping. Small nuggets of windscreen glass from its shattered eyes were clustered all around it.

"Oh my God," muttered Dushma, hand to her mouth, still too shocked to be angry at the trick that had been played on her. "What is it? What *happened* to it?"

"You haven't got a clue, have you?" smirked the boy, shaking his head. "You really haven't got an earthly. It's an elidra. An electric dragon. They built them to guard the tunnels, track down fugitives like us. But –" he sniggered – "they don't work. Beltrowser says the batteries just aren't big enough. Sometimes they electrocute a mouse, but that's about all they're good for. They can't control them properly either. Sometimes they'll go too near a station and then they'll have to close it off 'cos they're supposed to be a secret."

"Who can't control them?" asked Dushma, struggling to take all this in.

"So actually they're a real nuisance. Serves them right. And every now and again, when they're not too busy, they have to come down and hunt them. Can't be that many left now." He stepped round her and kicked the remains of the elidra. The carcass rattled like a wardrobe full of bare coat hangers.

Dushma trailed after him down the tunnel. "Wait a minute … who does? Who hunts them?"

"*Who?*" echoed the boy over his shoulder. "You really don't know anything, do you. The spugheads, of course. The frogging *spugheads*." He shook his head. "I don't know why on earth they're wasting their time chasing *you*. You're obviously completely clueless."

Dushma didn't know how much longer it took them. She lost track of time altogether, conscious only of the burning sensation in her exhausted legs and the need to keep within sight of the bobbing shadow in front of her.

She was worried that if she stopped he might not wait for her, or come back to look for her if she fell behind or lost her way. A couple of times now when he'd stopped to get his bearings she'd caught him looking at her, shaking his head and muttering, "What have I gone and done?" and "Useless," or, sometimes, the mysterious phrase he'd used before: "Ibmahuj is going to kill me."

"Oh, shut up!" she sobbed, the second or third time he did this. "I don't *want* to come with you, anyway. Why can't you just show me the way out?"

The boy merely shook his head pityingly and said, "This is the only way out."

Then she even thought about trying to retrace her steps all the way back to the station, but by that time they had already come a long way. What was more, their route had involved such a labyrinth of tunnels, secret passages and hidden entrances that she had to admit to herself almost as soon as it had occurred to her that this idea was ridiculous.

At last they reached a section of tunnel with rails in it. Unlike the track Dushma had seen at the station where she'd boarded her train, this section looked rusty and unused.

"*That* one's the live one," said the boy, pointing at the central rail. "This one's OK." He slapped the sole of his shoe down on to the metal.

They followed the tunnel round in a gentle curve towards a soft yellow glow in the distance. The track began to straighten and Dushma realized that the light was coming from a platform up ahead. At first she was alarmed by this, but as they approached it became clear that the station was deserted.

The boy had to help her up on to the platform. She was too tired to manage it by herself. She leaned against a wall for support and looked around.

In contrast to the ones she had already seen, the station seemed a large and lavish one, although a little old-fashioned and unkempt. The ceiling was high, decorated with a colourful frieze and supported by a row of elaborate columns. But there were drifts of dust on the floor-tiles and the clothes and hairstyles of the people in the posters on the wall were very out of date.

"Where are we?" whispered Dushma.

"You'll see. Come on," said the boy, leading her towards a wide flight of stairs.

At the top they clicked their way through unmanned cast-iron turnstiles and into a vast and airy ticket hall. The ceiling was domed and as tall as a tree at its highest point. It was tiled in white and shimmered here and there with patches of what looked like sunlight, although it wasn't obvious where it might be coming from.

There were two or three unoccupied ticket windows, each with a gold-faced clock above it, and several archways leading off in different directions from the main floor of the ticket hall. Plants in tubs and hanging baskets were spaced around the walls and the faint sound of running water could be heard. The noise of their footsteps echoed hollowly back at them.

"Where *are* we?" repeated Dushma, still whispering. "And where is everyone?"

"Where are we?" mimicked the boy. "We're nowhere. We're off the map. This place, it doesn't exist." He pointed at a section of wall behind her. She turned and saw a plaque bearing the name of the station in enamelled capital letters, white on blue in a red circle. HITLER STREET, it said.

"Embarrassing, no, for London Underground? Or at least it was by the time they'd finished building it. So it was never opened. They airbrushed it off all the maps, cut it out of all the official records. Conveniently forgot about it. So now nobody knows it's here. Except for me, and Ibmahuj, and Beltrowser. And now you, of course."

PART
II

I

"It's ironic, isn't it," said Ibmahuj. "The name of this place, I mean."

He sat in a high-backed swivel chair in the station-master's control room, his elbow resting on a control panel covered in Bakelite dials and sliders. His hair and skin were dark and his eyes were large and intense. Around his lips and on his chin grew a faint downy beard in a shape like a heart. He couldn't have been more than sixteen or seventeen, but he held himself with an air of calm authority.

"Yes, it's ironic," he repeated. "Somewhere named after one of the world's greatest despots becomes a place of refuge for the scapegoats, the socially excluded on the likes of whom his hateful politics thrived."

Dushma found herself nodding, not really taking in what Ibmahuj was saying but lulled by the reassuring quality of his deep and gentle voice.

"He might go on a bit," Beltrowser had said. "But he'll know what to do."

The boy with the mouth organ had first taken her down a corridor off the central ticket area and into the kitchen. This was a large room, tiled in white, warmed by an old-fashioned enamelled cooking range. There were glass-fronted cupboards on the walls, an old leather sofa in the middle of the floor and, in one corner, an arcade game with its insides showing through an open panel in one side.

It was in the kitchen that she met Beltrowser. He had been sitting on a pine bench like a church pew; propped open on his knees was a heavy book called *Levers, Ratchets, Rods and Cogs*. He hadn't seemed at all surprised to see her.

"Manners, Susskin," he had said. "Aren't you going to introduce your friend?"

"I found her!" explained Susskin. "I rescued her!"

Beltrowser put down his book and uncrossed his legs. He was tall and bony, with prominent cheekbones, a mop of sandy hair and a dusting of freckles across the bridge of his beaky nose. His expression was distracted, as if his mind was still wrapped up in what he had been reading.

Dushma had learned to be relieved at not attracting attention. On the street when people looked right through you that was good. But now Beltrowser's indifference irked her for a reason she couldn't have explained. She found herself wanting to say something arresting and sophisticated to command his attention, but nothing came to mind.

"Well done," said Beltrowser to Susskin. "Whatever it was you rescued her from, it must have been truly terrible for her to choose to remain here even in the face of your overwhelming hospitality. Is she hungry, do you think, after such excitement?"

"You could have some toast, I suppose," said Susskin ungraciously, scraping at the floor with his toe.

There was a half-eaten loaf of bread on one of the worktops, and several open jars. Dushma hadn't had anything to eat all day and her stomach felt like a gurgling, knotted hosepipe inside her. She threw a grateful glance at Beltrowser, but he had returned to his book.

Susskin made toast on the electric range in the corner of the kitchen. He put the bread in a hinged wire griddle and held it under the lid of the hob until it browned. The toast came out criss-crossed with little square scorch marks where it had been pressed through the mesh. There was jam and peanut butter and Marmite and chocolate spread and Dushma ate several slices smothered in each of these while the two boys talked about her as if she weren't there.

"The point is, what's he going to say?"

"You should have thought of that, shouldn't you?"

"I did! I've been thinking about it all the way back."

"No, I mean…"

"But they'd got her, man! They were going to do her! I didn't have any choice. Listen: she's one of us, she isn't registered. It's extenuating circumstances. He's got to see that. I mean, *you* don't think I've put us in danger, do you?"

Beltrowser turned and gave Dushma his full attention for the first time. "Depends," he said, after a few seconds' careful scrutiny, "whether you were followed or not. And I must say, although she seems harmless enough she could always be a spy, couldn't she?" It was hard to tell whether he was teasing or not. "I admit it would have to be a fairly unlikely combination of coincidence and elaborate planning, but it's not impossible, is it? I mean, she could be wired up like a pylon for all we know."

"Oh." Susskin frowned, and then a slow and cunning grin began to spread across his face. "But we know how we could find *that* out, don't we?"

"Whatever we do, we'll have to wait until tomorrow to hear what Ibmahuj thinks. He said he'd be back late."

"Exactly! You see? Double standards or what? *You* know where he goes. You know as well as I do where he is right now! He's with that, that … creature, that *hussy*. But now I've brought someone back he'll give me grief."

"Bringing someone back is different. We decided no one would do that unless we'd all agreed to it beforehand."

"I *told* you, there wasn't any time! But listen, I've had this idea. I've told her to say she's from some resistance movement somewhere. An underground cell, like us, or, or … a cadre! That'll sound good. I mean, she might be anyway, mightn't she? I've told her otherwise he might throw her out. Me too, maybe. The trouble is, she'll have difficulty sounding convincing 'cos she knows absolutely nothing at all."

Her energy restored, Dushma had been waiting with increasing irritation for a chance to interrupt. Now her patience had run out and she pushed her chair back angrily. "Will you both stop talking about me like I'm somewhere else? I've told you already I've got no intention of pretending anything. Especially when I've got no idea what on earth you're on about."

Beltrowser looked apologetic. "I'm sorry," he said. "Take no notice of Susskin. He's being melodramatic. No one's going to get thrown out."

"And I've already said to him, see if I'd care anyway. If you want me to go just show me the way out, that's all. And who is Ibmahuj? Is he supposed to be in charge?"

"Huh. He's not supposed to be. No one's *supposed* to be. He thinks he is, though. Can't imagine why."

"He does usually seem to know what we should do. But we don't really have a hierarchy here. Or rules, as such. The idea is, everyone agrees to do what's best for everyone."

"*Oh* yes, that's the *idea*, and very nice too it sounds in *theory*, but you know as well as I do that *actually*..."

"Now come on, be fair. We don't just follow his suggestions all the time. What about when you wanted VoltRage 5000? He didn't mind us going ahead with that, did he? You have to admit..."

Childishly, Dushma felt the urge to bang the table in order to get their attention. "What's VoltRage 5000?" she demanded, more to try and assert herself than because she really wanted to know.

"Do you really want to know?" asked Beltrowser keenly.

"Nothing! Didn't I tell you? She knows *nothing*."

Beltrowser nodded proudly at the arcade game standing in the corner. "She wouldn't know this one even if she's played the original. I've hacked around inside it a bit. It's the new improved mark two."

"That's right. Great fun. Want a go?" Susskin smirked.

Now that they were both staring expectantly at her, Dushma felt uncomfortable. She had never played an electronic game. The only ones she'd ever seen up close were the ones in the takeaway shops that she and Alison Catfinger sometimes visited. They had held no attraction for Dushma, although Alison was always fascinated by the pinball machines. She would lean against the clunking, flashing table when someone else was playing in the hope of being asked to join in.

"You play it with your hips, honey," she'd once explained loudly and suggestively to Dushma while they'd been standing at the counter. There was a new assistant in the shop, a dark and handsome youth that Alison wanted to impress. "You're a bit skinny for it, Dush. Hey, more batter on that cod, Luigi, she needs to put some weight on."

Even if she'd ever had enough extra money for a game, Dushma would rather have spent it on a can of Coke or some chocolate. So she wouldn't have been interested in the offer Susskin made, even if the forced casualness of his tone hadn't made her suspicious. As it was, the knowing grin he now wore reminded her uncomfortably of the expression on his face when he'd invited her to step ahead of him round the corner and into the wreckage of the elidra.

She took a deep breath. She was tired but she wasn't going to let herself get worked up. She had no proof they were trying to trick her, and after all they had given her something to eat. She was about to make a stiffly polite refusal when Beltrowser intervened.

"Wait a minute, that's not fair. I think you should warn her first."

Susskin stopped trying to look nonchalant and burst into a schoolboyish snigger. "Ohhhh go on, it's harmless, just a bit of fun. And anyway, I didn't know, that time you first got me with it!"

Dushma felt herself colouring. "Warn me? What about?"

"I've electrified the console," explained Beltrowser. "If you're losing you get a shock. Or a few. I mean, it's totally harmless, they're very light… Well, OK, if you're really getting pasted it might sting a little bit… But it shouldn't be that dangerous, as long as you're not wearing a watch, or any rings. Not to mention any kind of hidden microphone…"

"And you were going to try and make me play it? Without saying anything?" Though she struggled to control it, Dushma heard her voice beginning to rise. "What is it, some kind of a test? Or is this your idea of a practical joke?"

Susskin had stopped laughing and was staring crossly at the floor. "Bet her hair would've stood up really good," he muttered sulkily.

"Look, of course you don't have to if you don't want

to," said Beltrowser. "We're not used to guests and... Look, let's just forget it, OK? I'm sure he didn't really expect you to..."

But Dushma had risen to her feet. She knew she should force herself to laugh it off. Failing that she should just walk away. But they wouldn't tell her the way out. And she was tired, and angry, and she wanted to prove that she wasn't afraid, and that she didn't have anything to hide. And she wanted Beltrowser to be impressed.

"Come on then," she demanded. "How do you play?"

II

Dushma had done so much that day that she thought she would fall asleep immediately. Instead she lay awake for a long time, too exhausted to relax, random images from her recent adventures flashing past her closed eyes.

Susskin had shown her to a room with three bunk beds set into the wall. No one else used the room so she chose the topmost bunk.

"For the nightshift," Susskin explained. "Nice and cosy. You should be warm enough, even though I don't suppose you remembered to bring a nightie."

It was true that Dushma hadn't thought of this. Embarrassed, she avoided his eye.

The bunk itself, once she was in it, reminded her of what she had always thought it must be like to sleep at sea. It was as if she was tucked up on a high, narrow shelf. There was a hardwood lip to prevent her rolling out, and the ceiling was only centimetres from her nose. If she sat up in the night she would bang her head. There were brass hooks for her to hang her clothes from, and a round brass-framed mirror hung on one wall like a porthole. If she listened carefully she could hear a steady throbbing like the sound of mighty engines.

A heavy curtain ran the length of the bunk so that she could shut out draughts, but she found it too dark with it fully closed. She left it open so she could see the faint glow beneath the door from the exit sign in the corridor outside. She was so dizzy from her tiredness that the bed seemed to surge upwards and recede beneath her as she breathed.

How must she have appeared to Beltrowser, she wondered? She tried to recall what he had said to her. He had been polite, it was true, and apologetic on account of Susskin. But he had never lost his air of reserve and she couldn't help feeling that he would have preferred it if she hadn't appeared at all, and he could have been left in peace with his book. She was sure he wouldn't even have thought to ask her name, if she hadn't got fed up with being referred to as "she" and "her" and told them what it was. Probably rather haughtily, she now thought.

And then she had ruined everything by pig-headedly insisting on playing that space invaders game. Now he must certainly think that she was nothing but a hot-tempered show-off with no sense of humour.

She curled and stretched her fingers. Her palms still tingled pleasantly from the feel of the console under her hands. It had been exhilarating. She had had no idea she would be so good at it. She recalled the screen, swarming with explosions.

She turned over to face the wall and closed her eyes. Orange clouds like balls of flame seemed to be rolling slowly across the insides of her eyelids.

She remembered the time she had nearly set the viaduct alight.

It had been a few years ago, the first and only time she had ever tried to use an electric iron. Auntie Megan had always ironed her clothes for her up till then, but it was around this time that she was becoming more bitter towards Dushma, complaining that she didn't do enough to help. So early one evening, when Auntie Megan was out, Dushma had set up the ironing board and plugged in the iron.

First she had tried a white nylon blouse with an embroidered collar. She started with the back because that seemed easiest. Of course she knew that you shouldn't leave the iron too long in one place, so she moved it quickly back and forth, enjoying the slide of the hot metal across the smooth material. But despite her care she soon smelled burning. She hastily lifted the iron and stood it up on its heel on the ironing board but it was too late. The blouse had caught fire.

She seized it by the collar and flapped it in the air as if to shake the flames free, but this merely had the effect of oxygenating the blaze. Already she could feel the heat on her knuckles. Black shreds of burned nylon swirled around her and an acrid stink filled the air.

Face averted, she ran the length of the living room, flung the window open and dropped the burning garment out. She watched it fall, smoking and fluttering, down towards the rotating blades of the underground ventilation shaft. Long before it could catch the updraught and begin to rise again, the blouse had shrivelled away to a skeleton of sooty threads that were soon blown out of sight.

Then, when she turned away from the window, Dushma saw the iron glowing in the dusk like a pointed window in a burning church. Even from the far end of the living room the heat it threw out warmed her face. She had stood motionless for a long time, watching it as the glow faded and listening to the ticking sound it made as it cooled.

Now, drifting off to sleep in her bunk in Hitler Street, she thought how odd it was to be here, so deep beneath the ground, when every other night of her life had been spent so far above street level in her bedroom in the arch of the viaduct.

The following morning she woke and dressed and made her way back to the kitchen. She had no watch, but she assumed she had slept for a long time.

The kitchen was empty, though the loaf and the jars of various sorts of spread were still out on the worktop next to the electric range. She decided it would be all right to help herself.

She put two slices of bread into the griddle that Susskin had used. Then she raised the lid of the hob and slid the griddle underneath. Though she only held it there for a second or two, far less time than Susskin had needed, when she pulled it out again the bread was already almost too scorched to eat. She wafted the griddle through the air to try and dissipate the smoke.

A few minutes later Beltrowser came in. He was carrying a soldering iron, a toolbox and a roll of green and yellow striped wire.

"Good morning, Dushma," he said cheerfully. "How did you sleep?"

As he unpacked his toolbox on the table beside her, Dushma realized that she had suddenly become incredibly self-conscious about her every movement. She seemed to be watching her own gestures as if from another viewpoint. She had to think very carefully about even the most automatic action like taking the top off a jar of jam. She saw her hands on the lid as if they were someone else's. She vowed to stop biting her fingernails.

Once she had finished her breakfast Beltrowser took her to the station-master's office. She found she wasn't nervous at all. She had already decided what she was going to say to the mysterious Ibmahuj. She would tell him how grateful she was to Susskin for rescuing her from the ticket inspector, and then she would politely ask to be shown the way out. She had decided she would go and see Alison and ask her to cut her hair. She was proud of her long dark tresses, but was worried that they made her too conspicuous. Then she would make a careful reconnaissance and see if it looked safe to return to the flat in the viaduct.

The door to the station-master's office was made of dark wood and frosted glass. Written on it in gold letters were the words PRIVATE: STATION CONTROL.

"He'll ask you lots of questions," said Beltrowser. "Just answer them as best you can. He might go on a bit, but he'll know what to do." Then he knocked and walked straight in.

The office was gloomy inside. There were panels of switches and dials around the walls. Red lights glowed and winked. On the far side of the room was a window through which could be seen, a long way below, the lighted platform and the gleam of railway lines. A lamp with a green glass shade cast a pool of light on a table scattered with papers.

Ibmahuj sat by the table in a swivel chair. "What did she get?" he asked.

"A hundred and seventeen million," said Beltrowser. "And then it blew a fuse."

"Remarkable," said Ibmahuj, his fine eyebrows arching up his high forehead.

"I know. It was triple insulated. I can't think what could have gone wrong. I'm going to take the back off and have a look now."

"Let me tell you about our little community here," began Ibmahuj when Beltrowser had gone.

He explained how the station had been abandoned in the thirties when its name became too much of an embarrassment. "By the end of the decade, it was thought best to hide the fact that Britain had been building a station called Hitler Street as an act of appeasement. Such knowledge might have demoralized our allies and given encouragement to the enemy. Or perhaps certain influential people thought it might make a nice insurance policy. An ingratiating present for the victorious Führer. And if that's the case I'd very much like to know who those people were. Do you know why?"

Dushma shook her head.

Ibmahuj leaned forward, showing his teeth in a thin white line. "To blackmail their descendants, of course. Squeeze them for every treacherous penny."

He watched Dushma carefully for her reaction.

"Of course," she replied impassively.

Ibmahuj sat back again and nodded to himself. "Anyway," he went on cheerfully, "whatever the reason, now we've got the place to ourselves, and very comfortable it is too, I'm sure you'll agree. We've made a few improvements, as you'll see when Beltrowser shows you round. But tell me a little about yourself first of all."

He was easy to talk to. She found herself quite uninhibitedly revealing things that she would never have mentioned to Alison Catfinger, for fear of not seeming worldly or self-sufficient enough. Alison, she felt sure, would have seen her difficulties with Auntie Megan as a sign of weakness. But it was easy, even a relief, to explain the details of her domestic situation to Ibmahuj.

"I can't even remember my mother," she confided. "She

died when I was really young. I haven't even got a photograph of her or anything. Auntie Megan promised she'd look after me, but when it started getting difficult to make ends meet I think she regretted it. Every year she's turned a little bit sourer. But she wasn't always like that. She was a help to my mother and me, even though she wasn't really my aunt. They met at a protest camp, the same one I was conceived at, Auntie Megan said. In a thunderstorm. I don't think I was planned. Before she got too bitter to talk about her, Auntie Megan used to say my mother was a free spirit, someone who needed protecting from herself. So she took her under her wing. Then me too, when I came along. There's a phrase they use, isn't there, for people conceived on protests? 'Children of conscience'. I felt proud to be one of those, when I found out. I wanted to know all the details, but Auntie Megan got really evasive and I thought she must be hiding something. Now I'm sure it was just that she wasn't as nice to my mother as she liked to make out. I think she talked her into doing things she'd rather not've done. But when I kept on at Auntie Megan to tell me all the other things I was sure she must know, she wouldn't say anything else. Then she started telling me I was ungrateful. 'What's the matter,' she'd say, 'aren't I good enough for you?'"

"She does sound a bit difficult."

"Oh, it wasn't always as bad as that. It was only later she got like that. She used to be fantastic sometimes. We used to play cards. She'd do all these different impersonations and play a hand for each of them. There was the colonel, the vicar, the dowager duchess, the cowboy, the film star, the mafia *capo*… She'd say to me, 'Who would you like to invite tonight?' It was like being with a whole roomful of people. And the place was brilliant, under the viaduct. You really should see it! You can see for miles when the weather's clear. So I suppose it could've been much harder. But do you know the worst thing? The worst thing is, I don't even know what she was protesting about!"

"Sorry … who?"

"My mother! When I was conceived! When I asked Auntie Megan she said she couldn't remember. She said she was just there for the business. She could be so cynical sometimes."

"So what happened? You ran away?"

"I… They… Well, yes. Then they caught me with the wrong ticket, and Susskin rescued me."

Then he wanted to know what she was good at. She told him she could play the guitar, a bit. But could she make things, he asked, or grow things, perhaps? She had to admit that she didn't do much in either line. In that case, what *did* she do all day?

"Well, I like to read a lot," she said defensively. "We've got an encyclopaedia and I'm working my way through it alphabetically. And I walk around quite a bit. I explore. I like old churches." A thought suddenly struck her. "And I can ride a skateboard, too. A bit."

"So, you walk around a lot," said Ibmahuj, leaning

forward in his chair. He rummaged through the papers on his desk and picked up an *A to Z*. "Suppose I want to go from … from St-Beetles-in-the-City to, say, Holystoats Close in Soho. Avoiding the main roads, of course."

This was easy. Despite having decided that she didn't want to stay, Dushma was relieved not to be found totally wanting. Almost automatically she began to reel off the list of streets. As she named them, vivid pictures of cobblestones and brick walls sprang into her mind. "You'd go down Marlowe Street and along Dockside, then you'd go Tavern Road, Gutter Street, Slip Street, Twokiln Arches, Underground Mutterings, Splash Alley, down Mortar Way, into Can Street, turn right and there you are."

Ibmahuj was nodding to himself. After a long pause he clapped the *A to Z* shut and said, "We have no rules here. You might call our little community an anarchy, in the political sense of the word. Everyone is expected to make a contribution in order to share in the contributions of others. All important decisions are reached by consensus. But I'm sure there'll be no objections from the others about welcoming you into our number."

He took a key from his pocket and unlocked a drawer down by his feet. "You'll like it here if you're fond of exploring," he said, spreading a large, hand-drawn map out in front of Dushma. "These are the tunnels and shafts that link the underground system. A lot of them were used when it was being built and have simply been forgotten about. We're sure we've only found a fraction of them, so far. You wouldn't believe the places you can get to: museums, churches … fancy a midnight feast in the crypt of St Gotha's? It's on there, see it?"

Dushma bent over the map. It was meticulously drawn in different coloured inks. Hitler Street was in the middle, and around it were scattered other underground railway stations, most with names she recognized. They were linked by a network of lines of varying widths and shades. Some of these had been given names: Deep Street, Long Crawl, Crabwise. Others ended in an oval icon like a manhole cover, presumably representing an exit to street level. At various points on the map the illustrator had included sketches, either as decoration or to identify salient features of a particular area. Beside St Gotha's underground station was a manhole cover and a picture of cathedral spires. Near Battersea Park, smoke curled from the four distinctive chimneys of the power station. There were cobwebs, mice and, at a junction labelled "Dead Dragon Corner", the head and raised claw of an elidra.

"Keep that, you'll need it," said Ibmahuj. "And I'm sure you don't need me to tell you how careful to be with it."

"Thank you." Dushma began to fold up the map. Perhaps she wouldn't make her speech about wanting to leave. Not just yet anyway.

"The more you can memorize of it, the better. You'll find it comes in very useful for planning a speedy retreat after, say, a trip to gather provisions."

"Will that be part of the contribution I'm expected to

make? What does that involve exactly?" asked Dushma cautiously.

Ibmahuj spread his hands wide and shrugged. "We're very fortunate in the facilities we have here," he said. "We're able to live very comfortably in many respects, as you'll see. But unfortunately we're not entirely self-sufficient. Sometimes it's necessary for us to fend for ourselves, to survive by whatever means..."

"Do you mean you *steal* things?" interrupted Dushma, wide-eyed. She had never stolen anything, even when Alison had teased her for her timidity. It was all right for *her*, she used to think. Auntie Megan was always reminding Dushma that the penalties for unregistered juvenile delinquents, not to mention anyone who harboured them, were far more severe than for ordinary children.

"We don't think of it as stealing," said Ibmahuj. "We think of it as reparation. We are the unregistered. The dispossessed. What we take from society is a mere fraction of what we could have put back into society had we not been denied the chance, through no fault of our own, to contribute to the good of the community as hard-working, law-abiding, registered citizens." He noticed her uncertain expression. "Don't worry. You won't be on your own. The others'll look after you. I'm sure you'll be an asset to the community. I'm very glad you came." He extended his hand towards her, holding her gaze with his large, sparkling eyes.

"So you're not mad with Susskin?" Dushma asked, taking his hand.

Ibmahuj flashed his white teeth in a brief but dazzling smile and shook his head. "Susskin likes to be melodramatic. He knows there aren't any rules or punishments here. Sometimes I think that given his background he'd be more at home as a member of a rigid hierarchy. He likes to have something to rebel against. But underneath that cynical exterior he's fierce as a tiger. Sometimes when we've been out in the tunnels at night I've had to hold him back. He'd always much rather jump right into the middle of trouble than wait and hope it'll just walk away."

Ibmahuj rose to his feet. "There's plenty to do here. You won't find yourself getting bored. There are games to play, as you already know. And another thing we've got into the habit of doing is telling each other stories. We always try and make the time for that. Susskin is telling one in a day or two. His are usually based on his time at public school. They're always interesting."

"I never went to school," said Dushma.

"You'll be glad, when you hear the kind of thing Susskin had to go through. But they can be about anything you like. I hope you'll want to come along, and maybe contribute with one of your own, when you're ready."

III

"I got the mirrors from the platforms. They put them on corners so people could see if someone was waiting round the bend to ambush them. And the motors and cogs are from the storeroom."

Beltrowser was showing Dushma around the station. He was charming but a little distant, as if he'd really rather be doing something more important. Dushma was finding it difficult to break down his reserve without being too blatant.

They were standing in the ticket hall beside a machine that looked like a mechanical globe. But instead of a map of the world, the low metal frame supported a hemispherical mirror. Directly above the mirror, a shaft ran vertically up through the roof of the dome. Craning her neck, Dushma could see a patch of blue sky at the top of the shaft and a spark of light that looked like another mirror.

"The sunlight gets reflected down the shaft," Beltrowser explained. "Then this mirror here is linked to an electric motor by these cogwheels. The gear ratio's really low. You can probably hardly see it moving. But it's set up so that in one day, it shines the sunlight through three hundred and sixty degrees. It gives these plants around the walls enough light to grow."

He gestured round the ticket hall, indicating the tubs and hanging baskets which Dushma had seen the evening before. Looking round, she noticed a patch of light shimmering on the far wall. She reached out her hand towards the hemispherical mirror and watched the giant, blurred shadow of her fingers moving across the tiles.

"This is amazing," she said enthusiastically, bending to peer into the quietly whirring machinery underneath the mirror. "Did you build it all yourself?"

"Well, most of it. There's books that tell you how to gear your motor right. The workshop here is really well equipped for doing this sort of thing. I suppose it was in case they had to mend the points or fix the signals. I'll tell you what I'm thinking of doing next. I thought I'd try and build a fountain."

"That would be lovely. It'd be almost like being out of doors. D'you think it'll be difficult?" Dushma hoped she wasn't starting to sound too gushy.

"Well, we've got loads of running water here. The cistern's fed directly from the ring main. So I could just run a pipe across the floor from a tap somewhere. But I thought it might be more fun to try something a bit more challenging, like maybe an Archimedes screw, you know?"

"Oh yes, I know," said Dushma, nodding eagerly.

"Really?" Beltrowser smiled and raised his eyebrows in polite scepticism, as if he was worried that he wasn't being taken seriously.

"Yes, it's a … a sort of long propeller, like one of those bits of pasta, what are they called, fusilli. Only bigger."

"Yes, that's right. How did you know that?" Beltrowser's wide grey eyes were fixed on her with a greater interest now than he'd shown at any time since they'd met. Dushma glowed with pleasure.

"We've got an encyclopaedia at home. I was working my way through it." Then she admitted, "Actually, I only know about Archimedes because it was near the beginning. I never got very far. Shame really. Volume 12 was called 'How to Hug'. I always thought that sounded interesting."

She began to giggle and then turned it quickly into a cough when she realized that Beltrowser was not responding in kind. This was terrible. She was sounding like a hysterical eight-year-old.

"Really? Why was that?" he asked.

"Oh … I don't know. I just thought it did," she said lamely.

They left the ticket hall and made their way along passages and down stairs into the depths of the station. As they went, Beltrowser pointed out the most interesting and important places.

"That's the kitchen, you've seen in there… Next door is the laundry – we all just do our own whenever we need to.

The machines are ancient but they work a treat… And if you go further along here you get to the emergency exit: if you have to get out in a hurry just follow the signs."

They passed locker rooms, bathrooms and storage rooms, most of them unused. There was even a gymnasium, an echoing room with a hardwood floor marked out with coloured lines, ropes dangling from the ceiling and padded mats and a vaulting horse stacked up in the corner. "There's a badminton court," said Beltrowser. "Now we can play doubles."

"So when Ibmahuj says 'our little community'…"

"That's just his way of speaking. There's only us. We're hoping there'll be more soon, though."

"How long have you all been down here then?"

"Susskin's the most recent arrival. He's only been here a few months. Ibmahuj was the first. He's been here for ages. He went into hiding when his parents got deported."

"What? Deported? Why, what had they done?"

"Didn't he tell you? Well, I don't suppose he'll mind you knowing. They'd come from abroad you see, and set up a printing press in south London. It was a really rundown area, but they made a go of it. Did well, even. Within a few years they were employing ten local people. But then his dad stood for the council. So his rivals looked into his past and found he'd filled the immigration forms in wrong. And, as *everybody* knows –" Beltrowser smiled sarcastically – "illegal immigrants take jobs away from British people. His family were ordered out of the country. The printers they'd run couldn't carry on without them. It went bust and the workforce ended up on the dole. Now Ibmahuj wants to steal a printing press, set it up down here and circulate a samizdat newsletter on the streets. That's difficult though. Even a small press weighs far too much for us to carry on our own. So to start with he decided we... Well, anyway, we'll have to be a lot more organized before we can do that."

On the way back to the ticket hall they passed a heavy metal door with a wheel-shaped handle set into the middle of it. "What's in there?" asked Dushma curiously. It looked like the kind of door they had on submarines in wartime navy films. Doors like this always burst open in the final reel, unable to resist the weight of the black and foaming water behind them.

"In where? What, in there? Oh, nothing, just stores." For the first time during their tour, Beltrowser sounded evasive.

"Can I look?" Dushma had stopped and was trailing her fingers around the rim of the wheel.

"Well, actually ... it's locked and I haven't got the key on me. Come on, we're nearly done."

Beltrowser turned away and strode purposefully on down the corridor. After a few moments Dushma shrugged and hurried after him.

"So, what else do you know about Archimedes?" he asked her when she caught him up.

"Well, there's the story about the bath, of course," said

Dushma. She had been hoping for this opportunity, and immediately forgot the mysterious door. She gathered her nerve, swallowed and looked Beltrowser straight in the eye with what she thought was just the right combination of seriousness and flirtatiousness. "And I know he said that if you had a lever long enough, you could make the earth move."

IV

By the time Dushma had been at Hitler Street for two or three days she was starting to feel at home in her new surroundings, and had given up all thought of trying to return to the viaduct. The station was vast and complex, but she was now able to find her way to and from the most important parts without guidance. She was also, she thought, becoming accepted by her new companions.

Even Susskin was behaving more civilly towards her. He had gone as far as to offer her the loan of his personal stereo, an invitation which Dushma had accepted gracefully. But she didn't dare admit, when she returned it, that she had been unable to get it to play any music. She was still wary of his scorn.

At first she had wondered what they would do all day. It turned out to be not quite the right question to ask. By day they did little. It was only late at night, when the last trains had run, that they came forth and roamed the tunnels.

"You don't have to come, not if you don't want," Beltrowser told her, the first time she accompanied them.

"Oh. Won't I be useful?" asked Dushma.

They walked in single file along the track, Beltrowser leading, Dushma in the middle and Susskin bringing up the rear. After many turns and detours via narrow passages into different tunnels, the light from another station came into view round the bend in front of them.

Still in the shadow of the tunnel, Beltrowser stopped and turned to Dushma, a finger to his lips. He pointed to the security camera hanging from the roof above the end of the platform. "Watch this!" he mouthed at her.

When they had left Hitler Street a little after midnight, Beltrowser had been wearing a dark blue beret. It had sat incongruously on his fine, sandy hair. Now he had it in his hand and was swinging it back and forth as if preparing to throw a quoit.

Leaning forward, his tongue sticking out in concentration, he tossed it in an upwards-curving arc out across the platform towards the camera. His aim was good: the beret caught on the protruding lens and stayed there, hanging by its stitched leather hem.

The three of them moved quickly out from the mouth of the tunnel and across the empty platform.

"Won't someone get suspicious, when they can't see anything?" Dushma asked.

"I told you. She knows *nothing*," muttered Susskin from behind them.

"I found a very useful booklet once," Beltrowser reassured her. "*Procedure and Practice for Underground Nightwatchmen*. It says that if they see anything unusual, they have to go and investigate. But if they can't see anything at all, they just sit tight and log the faulty camera in the maintenance book. And there's no reason she should be expected to know that," he added over his shoulder.

Halfway along the platform stood a chocolate machine. It was lit up from within and the pictures of the goods inside glowed softly on its curved plastic case. The chocolate was served chilled and inside the machine a refrigeration unit hummed and gurgled.

"Filled last night, according to the rota," said Beltrowser, patting its side.

"Not that it makes a lot of difference," said Susskin cuttingly. "He never gets much out of them."

"Are you going to keep watch or not?" asked Beltrowser mildly.

"Yeah yeah, all right, nothing coming."

"Seriously. I don't want an elidra breathing down my neck."

"Huh. Big deal. One good poke and they roll over. More than can be said for this thing, I bet you." Susskin kicked the nearest leg of the chocolate machine and wandered a few paces back up the platform.

Beltrowser was uncoiling a length of wire with a hook on the end of it. "Watch this," he said to Dushma, feeding the hook up inside the machine. "Now what you have to do is find the slot the stuff comes down through… Ah, there we are…" He crouched to give himself a better angle for pushing the wire upwards. "Now what I want you to do is… Can you put your ear against the front … bit further up … that's right. You'll hear the wire, but what I want to know is if you hear a twanging noise. Because that means I'm touching the spring, OK?"

"Boys and girls," announced Susskin sarcastically, "Joachim Beltrowser is a highly qualified professional cracksman. Don't try this at home."

"Really? Is that true?" asked Dushma, stifling a giggle.

"What? No, of course not," grunted Beltrowser. "Nobody runs courses on breaking into chocolate machines."

"No, I mean are you really called Joachim?"

The arrhythmic scratching of Beltrowser's hook sounded faint but insistent above the soothing hum of the machine's refrigerator. After the warm, close air of the tunnels the machine was pleasantly cool under Dushma's cheek. She closed her eyes and swallowed a yawn.

"He started off with gobstopper machines, you know," said Susskin conversationally. "He was better at those, but we got worried all our teeth would rot."

"Hear anything yet?" asked Beltrowser. "Try moving over to the left a bit."

Dushma slid her head sideways across the front of the machine. The humming noise in her ear grew louder. "I think you're here," she said, tapping the plastic casing by her nose.

Above the scraping sounds of the probing wire she heard a sudden, heavy clunk, followed immediately by a rushing, jostling sound. She sprang back from the machine in time to see the dispensing trough fill up with brightly wrapped confectionery. After a pause the machine hummed more loudly still and, with a rattling and a clinking, money began to drop from the reject coin slot in a cascade of coppers and silver.

Susskin was staring at the machine in amazement, his flippant attitude entirely gone. "Superstar. Just … totally superstar," he muttered, shaking his head. Then he pulled his rucksack off his shoulder and began scooping up handfuls of chocolate bars, fancy biscuits and packets of crisps.

"Well come on, don't just stand there," he snapped over his shoulder to Beltrowser, who was looking admiringly at the end of his wire hook. "Pick the coins up, man! Paydirt or what, eh?"

"D'you know what this means?" asked Beltrowser. "It means we're on a roll, that's what."

"Huh. Listen to him," snorted Susskin. "It means someone didn't close the machine up properly, that's all. I'd like to see how long it is before you get that kind of luck again."

"Luck's got nothing to do with it. It's practice, that's what it is. I'm getting better at feeling the springs. I could tell it was about to give. It's 'cos there are three of us." He smiled encouragingly at Dushma. "Having someone to listen really makes a difference."

"Huh. You never asked me to listen."

"Anyway, now I've warmed up I think I'm going to try a telephone."

"What? No way! Don't be stupid. You've never got anything out of a telephone."

"So? I haven't tried for ages. You're up for it aren't you?"

"I don't know. I mean, I suppose, as long as we're careful…" said Dushma. She was reluctant to be drawn into the argument, but keen to prolong her new role as Beltrowser's indispensable assistant.

"Of course we'll be careful. There's phones in the car park right above the station. There's a manhole cover next to them; we won't even need to go through the ticket hall. Come on, let's just give it five minutes, OK?"

They went up the emergency staircase, where there were no security cameras. Beltrowser led the way, explaining to Dushma how phones were much more difficult than vending machines, because the only way in was through the reject coin slot. Susskin trailed reluctantly behind them, carrying the rucksack full of rustling packets of sweets and chocolate. "It's not that I'm *worried*," he was muttering to himself. "It's just that it's completely pointless. And besides, I'm hungry."

Before they reached the top of the stairs they stopped beside a wooden panel set into the wall. There was no handle on it, but it wasn't locked, and Beltrowser was able to lever it open with the blade of his penknife. In a cavity beyond the panel was a vertical ladder, bolted to the wall.

One by one they swung themselves up on to its metal rungs and continued their ascent.

The smell was the first thing Dushma noticed as Beltrowser helped her out through the manhole cover at the top of the ladder. She peered around her, trying to work out where she was, nostrils filled with the familiar tang of damp concrete, spilled motor oil and stale exhaust fumes.

The car park was poorly lit. Of those lights that there were, several were smashed, and the others shone dimly out from behind smears of felt-tip pen. Yet even in the semi-darkness she recognized the loops of graffiti on the walls. This was her car park, hers and Alison's.

The manhole cover was close to the stairs that led up to the other levels. On a pillar in the shadowy stairwell were the four phones that she and Alison had sometimes checked for forgotten change.

"See?" said Beltrowser. "They're the old sort, too. Should be easier than the new ones. And I bet they haven't been emptied in years!"

"That'll be 'cos they haven't been used in years," said Susskin pessimistically.

It soon became apparent to Dushma that it was going to be difficult for them to repeat their earlier success. The metal casing of the phone was much thicker than the plastic shell of the chocolate machine, and it was almost impossible to hear the sounds of Beltrowser's hook as he probed the reject coin slot. The height was awkward too, and in order to listen properly she had to crouch and twist her neck. The buttons on the front of the phone pressed uncomfortably into the side of her face.

"Maybe I need a different ... *mmmf* ... a different kind of wire," grunted Beltrowser, crouched at her feet. "Trouble is ... it's either flexible enough, or strong enough ... but not *both*..."

A thought occurred to him and he paused in his efforts to thrust the hook further up inside the phone. "I know, what if I had something I could heat up, with a car battery or something. Then it'd be bendy when it was hot, but it'd get stronger again when you turned the current off."

The ridiculousness of their positions suddenly struck Dushma and she felt the urge to giggle. It was like one of those scenes from sitcoms on TV where the father or the husband walks in unexpectedly and completely misunderstands the situation.

"You've got two minutes left!" whispered Susskin from beside the manhole cover. Dushma moved her cheek to a slightly more comfortable position.

The phone rang.

Frozen with surprise, the three of them stared at it for several seconds. Its electronic burble echoed around the car park with what seemed like deafening insistence.

Susskin was the first to recover. "For God's sake shut it up!" he hissed.

Reflexively Dushma reached out and snatched the receiver from its cradle. The sudden silence seemed to rush back into her ear with a noise all of its own.

The receiver crackled in her hand. A voice was coming from the earpiece.

"What the hell are you doing? Just drop it! *Come on!*" Susskin stood poised for flight, his voice hoarse with urgency.

Dushma glanced uncertainly at Beltrowser but he was staring at his piece of wire again, this time with a look of incomprehension on his face. Slowly she put the receiver to her ear.

"Hello?" The voice was clipped, impatient and somehow familiar.

"Hello, who's that?" replied Dushma automatically.

There was a pause and then the voice spoke again. Dushma felt her throat tighten as, too late, she recognized who it was.

"Why good evening, young lady. What a pleasant surprise. And how are you enjoying life on the run?"

Dushma opened her mouth to speak but the only noise that came was the dry sound of her tongue unsticking itself from her palate.

"I think you should know," went on the voice, "that one of my constables broke an arm. And the other one's in a coma. His relatives are beside themselves. So you see, there can be serious consequences to resisting arrest. But in your case it may still not be too late. I'm sure we could come to some arrangement, if you decided to be sensible. That's right my girl, we might just let you off, if you cooperate. Think about it, won't you?"

The phone went dead in her hand. Slowly she lowered the receiver. What should she say? What would the others think, if they knew who had been speaking to her? What if they decided it was too dangerous to have anything to do with her? How could they possibly believe it was merely the most fantastic coincidence?

Curiosity overcoming his caution, Susskin had left his position by the top of the ladder. "Come on then, who was it?" he demanded.

He noticed Dushma's hand trembling as she replaced the receiver. "Hey, it wasn't one of those bloody perverts was it? Give it here, I'll tell 'em…" He seemed about to snatch the phone back up from its hook.

"No, no," said Dushma hastily, laying a hand on his arm. "Just a wrong number, that's all."

"Huh. Funny wrong number, that's all I can say. What time does he think it is?"

"I think he just wanted … a pizza, or something."

The creak of a door sounded from one of the levels above them. Susskin and Beltrowser looked at one another.

"No cars left down here," said Susskin. "Could be a security guard…"

"They have security guards?" asked Beltrowser, looking round at the graffiti-covered walls.

"Dunno. We could scare 'em." Susskin peered round the pillar then ducked back again. A look of eagerness crossed his face. "I know! Let's do the terrorist trick!" Now that actual danger loomed he seemed to have forgotten his earlier eagerness to flee.

Another door creaked, and now footsteps could be heard

approaching down the stairs. Beltrowser shook his head. "Whoever it is, they're not in a hurry. I think we've got time to make a run for it."

Darting from the shelter of the pillar, they sprinted across the oil-stained concrete and scrambled one by one down the ladder. The last to descend, Susskin drew the manhole cover back into place as quietly as he could.

Almost tumbling over each other, they spilled out on to the emergency staircase, bounded down it three steps at a time and raced across the platform. Passing beneath the security camera, Beltrowser reached up without breaking his stride to pluck his beret from the lens. Only when they reached the relative safety of the tunnel did they pause to catch their breath.

"So will you *listen* to me next time?" panted Susskin, slumped with his back against the curved brick wall. "You're not going to get anything out of a phone. Even when you're on a roll."

"I've no idea what happened," confessed Beltrowser. He was still holding his wire hook. "Might've, I don't know, short-circuited it somehow, re-routed the call."

They rested for a few minutes, sitting on the floor of the tunnel and eating Kit Kats from the rucksack to restore their strength. After the sudden panic of their flight, Susskin and Beltrowser had soon recovered their spirits and were swapping jokes as they ate.

"Twelve-inch deep-pan pepperoni please!" said Susskin — rather suggestively, Dushma thought. "You should've pretended to be the speaking clock. That would've really wound him up!"

"No, next time get his credit card," instructed Beltrowser. "Then we can get our own in on his number."

Dushma found it hard to join in their levity. She was unused to being up so late and tiredness was beginning to overcome her. Every now and then the back of her neck tingled as if she was being watched. To try and take her mind off this unpleasant feeling, she asked, "So what was this terrorist trick you wanted to do?"

"Oh, that!" Susskin leaned forward, hunched his shoulders and covered his ears with his hands. "*Seven!* ... *Six!* ... *Five!* ..." he mouthed, as if shouting. Then he threw back his head and snorted with laughter. "Ha! You should've seen 'em run! Never seen a spughead move so fast in all my life. Works best if you're wearing a balaclava, though."

"Strictly for emergencies only, that one," said Beltrowser. "The tunnels were crawling for days afterwards. They were looking for bombs, of course."

"Takes a little imagination to survive down here you know," said Susskin smugly. He nudged Dushma. "Hey, you coming to hear my story tomorrow?"

"What? Oh, yes. Yes please."

"It'll be another school one, I suppose," said Beltrowser.

Susskin ignored him. "Oh, good, I was hoping you were. I know I shouldn't say so myself, but—"

"But you always do," interrupted Beltrowser.

"– but this one really is a frogging corker!"

They set off again. The quickest way home lay along the track, and they picked their way down the tunnel in single file, taking care to avoid the rails.

They hadn't been going for long before Dushma found herself lagging behind the other two. She thought of calling out, but didn't want to risk being seen as a liability on her very first expedition. So she lowered her head and struggled on, shuffling her leaden feet forward as fast as they would go, and supporting herself against the wall where she could so as not to stumble against the rails.

She had lost track of the time completely. Before they set out, Beltrowser had given her a cheap plastic digital watch and made her synchronize it with his own. "It's in case we have to split up," he explained. "So we can agree on a time to rendezvous." The strap was too loose and the watch chafed against her bony wrist. She glanced at it now and the display said 9.37a.m. That couldn't be right.

When she looked up again the other two were no longer in front of her. Panic squeezed her chest. Then she caught a movement out of the corner of her eye. A hand reached out from an alcove in the wall beside her and pulled her in. Before she could shout out another hand was pressed against her mouth.

"Can't you keep your eyes peeled?" she heard Susskin mutter angrily.

"There's something coming," hissed Beltrowser, his voice right in her ear. "Listen. Can you hear it?"

After a few seconds Dushma became aware of a faint

whirring noise from further down the tunnel. Then as she held her breath she made out an irregular scratching noise, almost imperceptible at first but gradually growing louder. The fine hairs on her forearms began to prickle.

"We're trapped," breathed Beltrowser.

"A decoy," whispered Susskin from behind them. "Create a diversion. It's our only chance."

"No, Susskin, stay where you are!" commanded Beltrowser hoarsely. "Look!"

The whirring, scratching noises were coming closer. Dushma leaned forward slowly and peered out of the alcove. At first the tunnel up ahead seemed empty. Then she caught sight of the glint of metal in the light of a lamp mounted on the wall nearby.

Something was moving towards them along the tunnel. Straining her eyes, Dushma saw a tapering silver head, pointed ears and dully glowing eyes. Then she noticed what could only be a pair of wings, half unfurled for balance and made from what looked like overlapping sheets of pearly white foil, strengthened by a framework of fine metal wires.

She knew without being told that this was an elidra.

The creature made its way slowly and slightly stiffly towards them, each movement accompanied by the sound of whirring motors from beneath its metal skin. Then it stopped and slowly lowered itself on to the live rail that ran down the middle of the tunnel.

There was a crackle of sparks and the smell of ozone filled the air. Slowly the elidra's drooping neck began to straighten. The glow in its eyes went from a dull red to a piercing, icy blue and its long, silver-scaled body rippled like a fish in a stream.

It's recharging itself from the current in the rail, thought Dushma. It was the most beautiful thing she had ever seen. She could feel Beltrowser's heart thumping against her shoulder blade. She hardly dared to breathe.

No longer moving sluggishly, the elidra reared up and sprang forward, its wings arched. It raised one taloned foreleg, undulating its claws up and down like a conjuror rolling an invisible coin across his knuckles. Then, moving faster than the eye could follow, it struck at something down between the rails.

When it raised its foreleg again, a small grey shape hung from its claws. By the light of its eyes, Dushma could see a mouse wriggling helplessly in its grip. But with its sudden pounce the elidra had used up most of its recently gathered energy. Before it could decide what to do with its prey its eyes dimmed and its neck began to sag. It lowered its foreleg and the mouse struggled free, disappearing into the shadows underneath the track. The elidra drooped tiredly down on to the rails again, the whirr of its motors falling from a high-pitched whine to a low, barely audible hum.

From behind her Dushma heard Beltrowser speaking; his mouth so close to her head that she could feel his breath in her hair.

"Listen. There's three of us. We could try and capture it. Now, while it's recharging."

"You are off your frogging bonce." Susskin spoke in a slow and deliberate whisper. "No. Way."

"But look, it's out of juice, it's helpless. We could take it apart, find out how it's made … maybe even make it work better."

"Don't you dare! It's a crazy idea and you know it. You know what? You're just showing off."

"What? What do you mean? No I am not!"

The elidra had been taking much longer to revive this second time. Now, its eyes still quite dull and its limbs clumsy, it hauled itself upright. Before Susskin and Beltrowser could argue further it began dragging itself away down the tunnel in a lurching parody of the lightning grace with which it had seized the mouse.

For a long moment after it had gone the three of them remained silent, huddled in their alcove.

"Well, that's that then," said Beltrowser at last, his casual tone sounding a little forced.

"Those things are bad news," said Susskin. "If I'd had a grenade I'd've taken it out." He mimed the motion of pulling free the pin. "Hunnerd and one … hunnerd and two … *kah-bam!*"

Beltrowser stepped sideways away from Dushma and out into the tunnel. He stood on tiptoe and reached his arms up into the air to stretch them.

Dushma hadn't realized how heavily she'd been leaning against him until he moved and she felt herself begin to topple over. She stepped back to try and recover her balance but her leg had gone to sleep and wouldn't support her. She would have fallen had Beltrowser not reached out and grasped her shoulder.

"Are you all right? Hey, you look exhausted. Why didn't you say something? Here, lean on me."

"No, lean on me," said Susskin.

"I thought you might leave me behind if I couldn't keep up," mumbled Dushma.

"What? No of course not, why would we do that? Where's the rucksack? Give her another bar of chocolate. That'll help her keep her strength up."

After a few minutes' rest they continued on their way, moving more slowly this time. Dushma still felt tired, but an emotion poised somewhere between apprehension and eagerness had replaced the gloom that had been upon her since the phone call.

Now her heart beat faster and she walked with a lighter step, her senses alert for the sharp, buzzy smell of ozone, or the sound of whirring motors and dragging metal scales.

V

Prenn-Pamflet, tough but fair head prefect of Melmerby School, leaned languidly against the Meissen-tiled wall of the sixth-form lavatories, two fingers thrust casually into the front pocket of his elegantly embroidered silk waistcoat.

"I've warned you, Cutt-Thump," he said wearily to the surly figure who stood before him, arms pinioned by two hefty prefects. "How many times is it now? Twice? Three times? Seems the old pi-jaw is a bit of a waste of breath in your case."

"Just keep it clean, Prenn-Pamflet," muttered the unrepentant Cutt-Thump, curling his lip disdainfully.

Prenn-Pamflet glanced at his fob-watch. The afternoon was slipping away and he was eager to return to the cosy comfort of his sumptuously carpeted study. Ensconced in his wing-backed leather armchair, he had been reading Thucydides in the original while his fag, Mome-Rathbone minor, toasted crumpets before the roaring fire.

He reached a decision. "You really must be taught, Cutt-Thump, to face the googlies of life with a straight bat. OK chaps, stuff his head down the toilet."

Flicking a speck of blotting paper from the sleeve of his immaculately tailored jacket, he watched impassively as the miscreant was dragged away. Soon muffled bumps and groans and the sound of flushing water began to emanate from the furthest cubicle as the prefects administered his tough but fair punishment. Ignoring the sounds, Prenn-Pamflet cocked his head towards the hidden speakers in the ceiling. "That's two terms running we've had Vivaldi in here," he mused aloud. "I really must see if I can't get them to play some Bach and raise the tone a bit."

Later that day, back in his study, Prenn-Pamflet heard a knock at the door. It was the clean-cut Templeton-Planet, deputy head prefect and—

"Wait a minute," Beltrowser interrupted. "I just can't believe there was ever anyone called Templeton-Planet. How come everyone's got some silly double-barrelled name?"

Susskin bunched his jaw defensively. "Why can't there be someone called that? It's my story, isn't it? How do you know anyway? It's not fair, nobody interrupts your stories."

"That's because with my stories people don't need to take a reality check every two minutes."

"No, wait a minute. You mean with your stories everybody knows they're never going to be able to understand them however many questions they ask, so there's no point trying."

Ibmahuj leaned forward in his swivel chair beside the station-master's control panel. "I think what Beltrowser meant," he intervened diplomatically, "was that your story is gripping enough in itself without you needing to make up implausible names for effect."

"It's not implausible, I checked! There's loads of Templetons in the phone book, and *nine* people called Planet. So if two of them got married, right, they might change to a double-barrelled surname, mightn't they?"

"'Specially if it was a shotgun wedding," said Dushma from her perch up on the ticket counter.

"Well, OK then," conceded Beltrowser. "But what if Templeton-Planet marries Prenn-Pamflet's sister? What are they going to call their children? It just wouldn't be fair on them, would it? Imagine the queues at the supermarket checkouts while people waited for them to sign their receipts. And how would the commentators cope if one of them became a football player?"

"Prenn-Pamflet hasn't got a sister!" shouted Susskin. He clenched the laboriously handwritten pages of his story tightly in his inky fists and shook them. "Now can I kindly get on with it, please? …Well, can I?"

Beltrowser shrugged and said nothing.

"*Thank you…*"

Later that day, back in his study, Prenn-Pamflet heard a knock at the door. It was the clean-cut Templeton-Planet, deputy head prefect and captain of the cricket team.

"Pitch is looking good for Saturday," he mused, loping to the mullioned window and peering out across the playing fields.

"So it should be," replied Prenn-Pamflet languidly, looking up from his leather-bound Thucydides. "Oate-Cribbins has been sneaking out every night for a week to douse the wicket in his special formula of Baby Bio, horse manure and percolated prune juice. Fancy a crumpet, old chap?"

"I say, it's a rum thing, what?" said Templeton-Planet, melted butter dribbling down his clean-cut chin. "I'm sure someone's been using the nets in secret. You know I like to chuck down a few dozen snorters before brekker? Well, for the last few weeks, no matter how early I've got there, there's always been fresh footprints at the bowler's crease. What d'you say to that?"

"There *have* always been."

"What's that? So you know?"

"No, there *have* always been. Fresh footprints. You said *there's* always been."

"Oh dash it all Prenn, give over, do. I say, not you is it? Practicing your deadly in-swingers and off-beamers?"

"Practising. No, certainly not. My early mornings recently have been chiefly occupied in contemplation of a particularly knotty postulate of Wittgenstein's."

"Oh yes, I know the cove. 'If lions could talk, we wouldn't have a clue what the blazes they were on about.' That's him, isn't it?"

"The very one. I find him just the thing to invigorate the mind after a cold bath has done same to the body."

"Well, whoever our mystery bowler is, more power to his arm, say I. We need to be on tip-top form for Scratchford Hall. They've been batting a blinder this season, apparently. Dubesley-Snaith saw them play against Wrexton College just a week or two ago. Wiped the floor with them. Formidable tail end."

Silence fell as the two prefects thought ahead to the forthcoming clash with their long-time rivals. The ormolu clock on the mantelpiece struck six. Abandoning all thoughts of returning to Thucydides, Prenn-Pamflet closed his book with a snap.

"So, homie, what's the word down in da barrio, or the sixth-form common room, as some people call it?"

"Well actually, that's what I came to tell you. I mean, it may just be all talk of course, but I think you should know there's gossip flying like wildfire already. You've put the cat among the pigeons now all right."

"What, pray, are you babbling about, dear chum?"

"Cutt-Thump, of course! He's not happy about this afternoon at all. He's been going around dissing your name and fomenting sedition all over the place. And he's vowed never to wash his hair again until he's had revenge."

"Ugh," said Prenn-Pamflet with an involuntary shudder of distaste.

"So… What was it he *did*, exactly, this time?"

"Consorting with Raquel Fairblush outside surgery hours."

"What, again? ...Well, I don't know, maybe he was ill."

"Then he should have called on Matron, not her assistant. No, the rules are quite clear. That's a privilege reserved for staff and senior prefects only, as he well knows. He's been warned before and he's got nothing to complain about. I was tough, but fair."

"Well anyway, *this* time the rumour is he's going to call you out. Bare-fist boxing behind the bike sheds."

Prenn-Pamflet shrugged phlegmatically. "I've been there before. He's nothing I can't handle." He looked down at his right fist and examined the mesh of fine white scars across the knuckles. His passage through the school had not always been easy, and the fearsome reputation that had helped him to the head prefectship was not unfounded.

"Don't be bonkers, Prenn! That was years ago. You're head prefect now. Nobody expects you to stoop to his level. Treat him with disdain, that's my advice."

"But I can't have him openly flouting authority. If he has to be made an example of, then I'm not going to shirk my duty."

"'Nuff respect, old chap, but don't underestimate the man," warned Templeton-Planet. "Cutt-Thump's a brute. He has a simian reach. And I understand his family are grocers."

"That in itself is nothing to hold against him," said Prenn-Pamflet reprovingly. "We're proud of our egalitarian principles here at Melmerby. I myself am only the Earl's second son, and so have had to make my way in life without any of the advantages my elder brother takes for granted."

"And you have no sisters, I take it?" enquired Templeton-Planet.

"That is correct," replied Prenn-Pamflet.

"Well, careful of your hands, that's all I can say. Don't want you crocking your fingers before the Scratchford match."

"Don't you worry. I'll bowl my overs if I have to do it with my arm in splints."

Templeton-Planet stood up and brushed the crumpet crumbs from his corduroys. "That's the spirit. I'm sure it'll all blow over, but if it doesn't, just tip me the wink if you need any help." He tapped the side of his nose. "I know a few people, know what I mean? If you want him blackballed at the tuck shop I can sort it out. Anyway, must dash old chap. Might get an hour or two at the nets before the light fades."

The door slammed shut behind Templeton-Planet. Prenn-Pamflet remained seated for a few seconds, then rose quietly, tiptoed across the room and turned the key in the lock. Then he went to his Chippendale roll-top desk and from a hidden drawer took out a stoppered bottle. He settled contentedly back into his armchair, bent his thoughts towards the beautiful assistant matron, Raquel Fairblush, and began to paint his nails.

Susskin paused and looked round at his three listeners. He picked up his glass of water and took a sip. Then he shuffled his pieces of paper slowly and deliberately. He had the air of someone who has their audience in the palm of their hand. He cleared his throat. "Part two!" he said.

The day of the Scratchford match dawned bright and early. Down at the nets, limbering up for his morning practice, Templeton-Planet snorted and stamped, whirling his arms in the air. Glancing down, he saw fresh footprints in the dewy grass by the bowler's crease.

In his rooms, Prenn-Pamflet was also awake, though not yet dressed. His hair still damp from his icy bath, he sat in his armchair in his stripy pyjamas, the *Tractatus Logico-Philosophicus* open on his knees. He barely glanced up when Mome-Rathbone minor entered with his breakfast on a tray. The room soon filled with the enticing smell of coffee and kipper croissants, a Melmerby tradition.

In her small but cosy room beneath the eaves of the sanatorium, Raquel Fairblush flung her window open. The rosy sunrise colouring her cheeks, she leaned out and began to brush her long and lustrous hair.

In the school basement, in the darkest corner of the boot room, Cutt-Thump was soaking his hands in vinegar. A scraping sound caught his ear and he looked up in time to see a figure creeping furtively between the lockers.

It was a skinny third-former in dressing gown and slippers, carrying a shoebox. He jumped when he noticed Cutt-Thump. The shoebox rustled and a set of trembling whiskers appeared above the rim.

Cutt-Thump straightened up and shook the vinegar from his fingers. He took a step forward and saw that the shoebox contained a hamster, crouching in a nest of tissue paper with its nose in the air.

"Oh, I say, Cutt-Thump, please don't tell," said the third-former, his voice quavering. "Prenn-Pamflet fed my last one to the headmaster's cat. He said pets were against the rules. He said he was being tough but fair."

"Don't worry, I won't say a word," Cutt-Thump reassured him. "But will you do a favour for me?"

It was already a hot day by the time the match began at ten o'clock. The white flannels of the players and the painted wood of the sightscreens glowed with an almost painful brightness in the sun. Most of the school had turned out to watch. The younger boys sat or stood around the boundary while the seniors and the masters relaxed in the shade of the small wooden spectators' stand. Many of them had taken advantage of the fact that the wearing of sunglasses was permitted at weekends.

A hush fell on the crowd as the last of the staff took their seats. The Melmerby headmaster's wife folded up her parasol and tucked it down by her feet, while her husband raised his brass opera glasses and watched the two team captains and the umpire walk out across the pitch.

Templeton-Planet won the toss and elected to bat.

"Good choice," murmured Prenn-Pamflet as Templeton-Planet buckled on his pads back in the pavilion. "The pitch'll get drier as the day goes on. The ball should be moving nicely by the time we're on to bowl."

"That's not the half of it, Prenn," replied Templeton-Planet with a wink. "The heat could make it uncomfortable for the Scratchford batsmen in more ways than one. I'll say this for Oate-Cribbins's secret formula: it don't half ponk when the weather's warm."

The morning's play did not go well for Melmerby. Their wickets fell steadily to the Scratchford pace attack, and by lunchtime their last man had seen his bails whipped off by a cunningly pitched off-break.

"It could be worse," reasoned Templeton-Planet, sitting on the pavilion steps after lunch and rattling the ice in his barley water. "It's a bowler's wicket. We should be able to pin them down. Pace from one end, some tricksy spin and swing from the other. What d'you reckon, Prenn?"

But Prenn-Pamflet was no longer beside him. He had caught sight of someone waving, and had risen and made his way to the top of the steps to where a nervously skipping fag was waiting for him.

"Message for Prenn-Pamflet!" squeaked the fag, his face half hidden behind an enormous pair of sunglasses. "Miss Fairblush says, can you spare a moment, she's got something she needs to tell you. She says she'll be in the san."

Prenn-Pamflet looked at his watch and then glanced back down the pavilion steps at Templeton-Planet. He hesitated, then hurried after the fag.

124

He still had not returned when, ten minutes later, the two teams stood ready to resume the game.

"We can't wait any longer," said the Scratchford captain. "This looks like it might be close, and we don't want to play the last few overs in bad light."

"Where's he got to, dammit," muttered Templeton-Planet. "I saw him not quarter of an hour ago." Dubesley-Snaith came running towards them. "No luck, Dubes? Did you try the san? I thought he might have gone for a plaster or… No? Goddammit then, where is he?"

"Haven't you got a twelfth man?" asked the Scratchford captain. "I mean, you're welcome to one of our chaps, but…"

Templeton-Planet reached a decision. "No, this is my best in-swinger. I can't believe he's going to let me down. We'll play with ten men until he gets back. Atkinson-Rambler, you drop back to long leg and I'll move a little bit squarer. I know it's a bit more running around but that should keep our field intact."

Prenn-Pamflet took the short cut to the sanatorium. There was no one in sight as he left the pavilion by the back door and jogged along the gravel path that skirted the headmaster's rose garden. As he turned the corner into the patch of open ground behind the bike sheds, he stopped. Someone was waiting for him on the far side of the clearing.

"Why, Prenn-Pamflet. How convenient," said Cutt-Thump, stepping out from beneath the trees. "There's something I've been wanting to ask you. Just what exactly is a googly, anyway?"

He raised his fists. The gentle breeze blew his lank, tangled hair into his eyes and he tossed it back with an impatient flick of his head.

Prenn-Pamflet nodded slowly. This wouldn't take too long. "Keep it clean, Cutt-Thump," he muttered, squaring his shoulders. As he advanced he wondered briefly why his adversary wore cricket whites.

Dubesley-Snaith had not been wrong in his assessment of the Scratchford Hall team. They played with caution rather than flair. Each new batsman took an over or so to acclimatize himself, solidly blocking each ball while he took the measure of the pitch and the bowling. But it wasn't long before they were snatching a single or a two from every other delivery, and Scratchford had soon amassed a considerable total of runs.

One factor in their favour was the unvarying nature of the Melmerby attack. Templeton-Planet was himself no mean bowler. He could muster a fearsome turn of pace and a high degree of accuracy. What he couldn't do was move the ball around the pitch, altering the length and speed of his deliveries to fool the opposition. He couldn't play games with the batsmen who faced him, tricking them into lashing out at a deceptively easy lob, or lulling them with a sequence of slower balls. A competent player who kept his nerve could soon anticipate the nature of each delivery and begin to make runs.

As a consequence of this, after only an hour or two of their innings Scratchford had almost overtaken Melmerby's score for the loss of only five wickets. The game was almost certainly theirs. The spectators were already beginning to drift away. Walking back to the mark at the start of his run-up, about to bowl what might be the final over of the game, Templeton-Planet was almost in despair. Then, glancing towards the pavilion, he saw the sight he had been hoping for since the start of play that afternoon. A tall dark figure in cricket whites was coming down the pavilion steps.

"Hold on a sec!" he shouted over his shoulder, and began to sprint for the boundary.

Long before he reached it he had slowed to a stumbling jog, his excitement gone. The figure on the steps was not Prenn-Pamflet.

"What's happened?" demanded Templeton-Planet. "Where is he? What's going on?"

Cutt-Thump's cheek was bruised, one eye was closing and dried blood caked his left ear lobe. The knuckles of his right hand were wrapped in a bloodstained makeshift bandage.

"Prenn-Pamflet isn't feeling very well," he said. "I'm afraid he won't be coming."

"*What?*" Templeton-Planet's breath came in heaving sobs. "Do you realize… Do you realize what the score is? Have you any idea what you've done?"

"Oh, I'm so sorry. Have I left you short of hoorays to

chuck the leather? Well, why not let me try to make amends and see what I can do?"

"How dare you? You've never bowled a decent over in your life! In fact I've never even seen you play cricket. Why, you … you … you're not even fit to blanco my pads! The people on this pitch are gentlemen! They'd sooner strike their own stumps than share it with a … a…"

"Suit yourself." Cutt-Thump shrugged and began to turn away.

His head dropping in resignation, Templeton-Planet noticed grass stains on Cutt-Thump's white cricket shoes. He remembered the mysterious footprints he'd been seeing every morning at the nets. He realized that his shoulder ached and that he really didn't want to have to bowl another over. He began to feel an obscure resentment towards Prenn-Pamflet for placing him in this situation. Why should he be concerned about whether or not it would be disloyal to his friend to allow Cutt-Thump to play?

"Oh, go on then, what do I care? Make a fool of yourself if you have to." With a dismissive flick of his wrist he tossed the ball away.

Instantly Cutt-Thump's arm shot out. The ball smacked into his palm as he snatched it eagerly from the air. His face a mask of concentration, he weighed the scuffed red sphere in his hand. He rolled his shoulders, wiggled his wrists and stretched his fingers carefully round the ball in the splayed grip of the spin bowler. Then without another word he strode past Templeton-Planet towards the crease.

"Round the wicket, six to come!" he shouted, breaking into a long-legged, confident run.

His first ball was pitched short and straight and Scratchford ran a two from it. Templeton-Planet shook his head as he watched the dispirited Melmerby wicket-keeper fumble the return from square leg.

The second ball was faster and longer and the batsman played safe and blocked it.

For his third delivery Cutt-Thump took an even longer run up, legs pumping like a sprinter. The batsman gathered himself for another defensive stroke but when released the ball travelled disconcertingly slowly: a gentle, tempting lob. Without enough time to change his mind, the batsman played defensively anyway and then looked annoyed at missing the chance of a boundary.

Cutt-Thump's run up for his fourth delivery was much shorter. As if all his energy was spent he ambled lazily to the crease, but on reaching it he uncoiled himself like a watch-spring to hurl the ball down the pitch almost faster than the eye could follow. The batsman had already moved forward in anticipation of another easy offering. Before he could lower his bat the ball had clipped the off stump and sent a single bail twirling high into the air.

"Oh, I say!" murmured one of the Melmerby fielders.

The next Scratchford batsman took his guard apprehensively. He was determined to be cautious, even when Cutt-Thump's fifth delivery sailed invitingly towards him. He stepped forward and planted his bat down firmly.

The ball bounced just in front of him and then jinked sideways as if tugged by a string. The batsman heard the stitching hum as it swerved past him and uprooted his middle stump.

His replacement was in no hurry for play to resume. He swung his arms about, loosened his shoulders, tightened his pads and adjusted the fit of his gloves. He tamped down a non-existent bump in the turf with his bat, then cocked his head and sniffed suspiciously. (A ripe and unusual smell now hung in the air near the wickets.)

Cutt-Thump waited at the opposite end of the pitch, flexing the fingers of his right hand and rubbing one side of the ball vigorously on his trousers with his left. When it was polished to his satisfaction he looked around at the positioning of the fielders.

The home team were visibly keener than they had been just a few minutes ago. The slips crouched lower and the outfield leaned forward on their toes. Waiting to begin his run-up, Cutt-Thump gestured to them to move inwards in anticipation of a catch.

"Round the wicket, one to come," said the umpire at last. "Play!"

Cutt-Thump bowled a full toss. The batsman drew himself up to take the ball on the volley but with one side smoother than the other it wasn't travelling straight. It caught the edge of the bat and flew sideways into the slips. Templeton-Planet flung himself down at full stretch, caught the ball and held it.

"*Owizzyorwoteyaaarrrrrrrrrrrrrrr!*" he roared in triumph, kicking his legs in the air.

This was the end for Scratchford Hall. A reinvigorated Templeton-Planet continued the attack from the opposite end of the pitch, and the last two demoralized batsmen lost their wickets in quick succession. Melmerby had won by a mere handful of runs.

The spectators erupted joyfully. The younger boys, knowing they would probably be granted a celebratory half holiday in the forthcoming week, cheered and threw their caps in the air, while shouts of "Bravo!" and "Well played!" rang from the seniors in the stand. Even the headmaster's wife joined in, holding her parasol aloft and flapping it open and shut in appreciation.

Templeton-Planet shouldered his way through the crowds of people streaming on to the pitch. "I say, splendid stuff!" he cried, clapping Cutt-Thump on the shoulder. "Coming for the post-match sandwiches? I'm sure the chaps will want to shake you by the hand."

Cutt-Thump shook his head, smiling with difficulty because of his bruised cheek. "I'm going to wash my hair. Then I'm going to the san to see if I can get something for this." He held up his right index finger. The first joint was red and swollen. "I think I might have broken it."

"OK, what did you think?" demanded Susskin triumphantly.

"Seriously?" asked Beltrowser.

"We have a rule," explained Ibmahuj. "No one says

anything about anyone's stories, unless the person who told it asks for an opinion. In which case you have to be totally honest."

"Yes, seriously," said Susskin, looking intently at Dushma. "What do you think? Nine out of ten? Forty-nine out of fifty? What d'you say?"

"Well … I'm afraid I don't know much about cricket," confessed Dushma awkwardly. "I'm not sure I quite followed it at the end. But what happened to the hamster, that's what I want to know."

"Er, I'm not sure… The hamster wasn't really very important…"

"Well, what *I* want to know," interrupted Beltrowser, "is why, if it was such hot weather, was there a roaring fire for toasting crumpets in his study?"

Susskin rounded on him. "I might have known. You're always the same. Splitting hairs and nit-picking. I'm surprised you don't take notes. 'What did you think of *Julius Caesar*?' 'Well, what *I* want to know is, how come he had that clock in his tent?' I give you depth and pathos, the dramatic unities of time and place, but you … you…"

"Keep it clean, Susskin," said Beltrowser, not without a hint of gentle mockery. "I didn't say it wasn't exciting enough, did I? I was just pointing out something any editor would've done, which is that if it's the middle of summer then no one's going to have a fire in their room, are they?"

But Susskin was beyond mollification. "You are *not* editing my stories! You know nothing about it. Haven't you read *Tom Brown's Schooldays*? How else is a chap supposed to grill his fag?"

He clutched his manuscript to his chest and glared round at the three of them. Then he twisted round, head down, wrestled belligerently with the door and lunged out of the room.

VI

Dushma and Beltrowser sat in armchairs in Beltrowser's workshop. It was an untidy room, full of tools and spare parts, yet it was cosy too. A long wooden bench ran along one side of the workshop. It was strewn with pieces of metal and tufts of wire wool. Files, pliers and soldering irons hung from hooks on the wall above it. A fresh pot of tea steamed at Beltrowser's elbow and a portable gas heater buzzed and sputtered soporifically in one corner.

There was a faint smell of motor oil in the air, which reminded Dushma of garages. Not the modern main-road service station sort of garage, but the little private garages that could be found down cobbled sidestreets, where Radio One played on an old tranny and men in boiler suits banged away at the innards of dismantled cars.

"I know I shouldn't tease him," Beltrowser said. "But he isn't usually so touchy."

"Does he always tell that kind of story?" asked Dushma.

"Yes. I think he's spent most of his life in places like that.

There are some characters I'm sure must be real: they come up time and again."

Dushma shook her head. "I just can't imagine it. D'you think that's how it really is?"

"I don't know. You remember that fielder, Atkinson-Rambler? He's been in before. In one story he hijacked a JCB in the middle of the night and ran amok. He demolished the sports block and dug up the headmaster's rose garden. I don't think Susskin was terribly happy at school."

"I never went to school," said Dushma.

"And I never went to schools like that."

"But his parents must have been rich, to afford to send him to somewhere like Melmerby. What happened? I mean, what went wrong? How did he end up here?"

Beltrowser shrugged. "Three strikes and you're out."

"I don't understand."

"He got expelled three times. When that happens they send you to special school. It's automatic. So Susskin ran away."

"And how about you? You went to school. You must have been registered too."

"Mmm," said Beltrowser unencouragingly. He smiled a quick, thin-lipped smile and looked away from her. Then he reached for the teapot, grasped the handle in his long fingers and swirled the contents absent-mindedly round and round.

Dushma could have bitten her tongue out for her

overeagerness. They had been getting on so well, but now she had clearly touched too soon upon a painful topic. Could she, should she tell him that she didn't care, that she would understand, whatever it was?

Beltrowser poured himself more tea and sat back with the mug pressed against his top lip. He stared off into the distance through rising coils of steam.

"Yes, I did really well at school," he said abruptly. "My parents weren't rich, they couldn't afford to send me anywhere. But I was lucky: the local comprehensive was a good one. The government told us their priorities were education, education and education, and if you'd seen the science labs that my class used to use you might almost have believed it.

"I loved taking things to bits, right from when I was old enough to crawl. My parents were terrified I'd kill myself: I couldn't see a plug without wanting to stick my fingers in it. I wanted to know how everything worked, and as soon as I could hold a screwdriver I started trying to find out.

"At school I was good at everything practical or technical: physics, chemistry, metalwork. I built a computer. It's not that difficult, there's books that tell you how. I just ordered all the bits and then put them together. It worked a treat. I couldn't've afforded one otherwise. I made little gadgets for round the house. Like a motor that closed the curtains when it got dark. It's so easy to get the bits you need: you just look in skips for old TVs or hi-fis.

They're full of printed circuit boards with useful parts on them. Look, I'll show you."

Beltrowser had become quite animated again. As if forgetting the original thread of his narrative, he put down his tea and began selecting things from a little rack of plastic drawers on top of his workbench.

"These are resistors ... I'll teach you Ohm's law if you like... And these are capacitors." Like a jeweller displaying his wares he placed the electrical components one by one on a square of folded newspaper in front of Dushma. They were shiny and brightly coloured and were mostly cylindrical or Smartie-shaped. Dushma thought they looked pretty, like sweets or tablets with angled wires sticking out of each end, although she didn't feel she ought to say so. If she'd found things like that in someone's rubbish she'd have wanted to keep them too, even though she had no idea what to do with them. She picked up a yellow capacitor and rolled it in the palm of her hand.

"And this is a chip." In his hand Beltrowser held a dark grey wafer, fringed with metal prongs like an insect's legs. "They're harder to find. I got that from an old computer. If I can find enough parts I might see if I can build another one."

He fell silent again and his expression became distant as he contemplated future schemes. More cautious in her prompting this time, Dushma asked, "I just wouldn't know where to begin. How did you find out all these things?"

"Well, I... Well, to cut a long story short, I got a place on a course. Well, it wasn't any old course, in fact. It was the applied robotics course at Imperial College. I was going to be the youngest student they'd ever taken. The competition for places was huge. It's the best robotics course in Europe. Maybe even the world, though apparently there's a good one at MIT."

He paused and twisted his fingers awkwardly around the handle of his mug. Dushma could see that he was worried she might think he was boasting.

"I have to mention that so you understand what it meant to me. It was what I'd always wanted to do. Robotics is fantastic. It's just the best bits of everything: computers, artificial intelligence, mechanics, electronics, hydraulics..."

He paused again. Dushma waited patiently for him to continue.

"Do you know what ROI is?" he asked, frowning at her suddenly. He pronounced it "Are Owe Eye".

"Republic of Ireland?"

"No. Well, yes, but it also stands for return on investment. How much you get back for what you put in. They usually use it when they're talking about stocks and shares, but you sometimes hear it in other contexts too, like training an employee, or even bringing up children. You know what I mean?"

"Yes, I think so." *She'll sell you for a bottle of gin*, Mr Mackenzie had said. That was Auntie Megan wanting her ROI for looking after Dushma.

"Well, the thing about courses like that one is that they're really expensive to run. The equipment you need for the lab work costs a fortune. And that's just to buy it, never mind the technicians you need to install and maintain it. Then there's all the raw materials you have to have for the practical work. And good lecturers are really scarce. It's not like an arts subject where all you need is a library and a pencil and paper. So the way they fund the course is by sponsorship from industry. Big companies put up the money and in return they get first refusal on the graduates. Fair enough?"

"I suppose so…" said Dushma slowly.

"Yes, sounds like the perfect arrangement, doesn't it? The college gets to offer a cutting-edge subject, the students get to study an exciting course and the companies get the workers with the skills they need. But because the companies are laying out all this money, they want to make sure they protect their ROI. They don't want to back a dud horse, one that might trip over before the finishing line. So they make you take a medical. They test your blood, take urine samples, check up on your family in case there's a history of mental illness. And they listen very closely to your heart."

Beltrowser tapped his chest. His voice was matter-of-fact, as if he was talking about somebody else. "In this case, they didn't like what they heard. They said my heartbeat was irregular. They couldn't tell why. The X-rays looked fine. But the upshot was they decided I was too much of a risk. They wouldn't let me have the grant."

"But that's not fair! You'd got a place, they couldn't just turn you away."

"That's life. The college was still perfectly happy for me to come. It's just that I'd've had to find the thousands of pounds in fees myself. And of course I couldn't do that. And after such a disappointment, I didn't really want to do anything else. I turned down all my other offers. I suppose I was still hoping there'd been a mistake. But eventually the only option I had left was to get a job. And when I wouldn't do that they took away my registration. It was the workhouse until I was eighteen, or drop out. So I ended up here."

He smiled and shrugged, appearing unconcerned, but Dushma noticed that his hands were shaking. "And what about your heart?" she asked. "Is it all right now?"

"No. It's thumping wildly." His throat moved as he swallowed. He reached out, took Dushma's hand and placed her palm against his chest. "Can you feel it?"

Dushma wasn't sure. Her own pulse was pounding so strongly in her ears that she found it difficult to distinguish Beltrowser's heartbeat from her own.

"Yes," she said, her mouth dry. She had no idea what was going to happen next.

Beltrowser moved his hand down over her bony wrist. His fingertips felt cool against the sore patch of skin made by the rubbing of her watch. "That looks a bit angry," he said. "I can get you some witch hazel for it, if you like." He undid the loose strap and laid the watch on his workbench.

Feeling suddenly confused and disappointed, Dushma lowered her arm back to her side. She watched Beltrowser's lean, precise fingers as he took a bradawl from his rack of tools, placed the point carefully on to the watch-strap and punched an extra hole in the textured plastic.

"It's slow," he said, noticing the display. "Maybe the battery'…" He shook the watch, then looked at it again. "No, wait a minute, the date's wrong. It's fast … three months fast! Did you try and change it?"

"No."

"Well, I don't know then… Perhaps it's been too near a magnet… Or maybe you're just living too quickly." Beltrowser twisted the back off the watch and peered inside. He touched the battery carefully and then snatched his hand back. "How weird… It's warm, hot almost."

He replaced the back and began to readjust the settings. "There must be something wrong with it. It's not a very good one. I'll try and get you another. There … it's right again for the moment."

Dushma concentrated on strapping the watch back on to her wrist. It fitted more tightly now.

"You know…" she began hesitantly. "About your course… Thank you for telling me that. I think it's really unfair, and … I'm sorry. Because, for a long time I've wanted to be able to go to school, so I think, maybe, I know a little bit how you feel."

She glanced up quickly through her eyelashes. He was

smiling at her shyly. His cheeks were pink. "Well, who knows. Maybe it was all for the best. The whole faculty was nothing but blokes. Probably wouldn't've so much as clapped eyes on a girl for the whole three years."

VII

Ibmahuj had boasted that London was theirs. That they could go wherever they liked. "Well, maybe not the room where they keep the crown jewels in the Tower, or Buckingham Palace, but pretty much anywhere else. You want to spend the night with the dinosaurs at the Natural History Museum? Sleep underneath the aeroplanes in the flight gallery at the Science Museum? We can take you there. We know where the tunnels are."

This evening they were going to St Gotha's Cathedral. There was a manhole cover in the crypt, Beltrowser said, and a secret ladder inside the walls ran all the way up to the base of the spire a hundred metres above the street.

Dushma and Susskin waited in an alcove in the tunnel some distance from the platform of Hitler Street. Ibmahuj had gone on ahead, and Beltrowser was locking up the station.

"There's security features," Susskin explained. "Beltrowser invented them. It's infra-red beams linked to a video camera. Just an ordinary one from Dixons, so we know if anyone's tried to get in. It's quite clever, I suppose. I told 'em what we really wanted was a deadfall trap. You know, like a tripwire that when someone falls over it a block of concrete overbalances on to their head. But no one would listen to me."

Dushma slipped her hand inside her satchel to make sure she had brought *Lives and Legends of Historic London* with her. It was her turn to tell a story, and she thought that the place they were going to would be a good location for the one she had chosen.

Susskin had pulled his headphones on and was fiddling with the controls of his personal stereo. After a few seconds he looked up and frowned at Dushma. "What've you done to this thing?" he demanded. "There's nothing but weird static on this cartridge now. It was one of my best ones as well."

"I'm sorry. Maybe I pressed the record button by mistake, or something."

Susskin seemed to be about to make a withering remark when his attention was distracted by something on the ground near his foot. Bending down, he snatched up a half-smoked cigarette and held it triumphantly aloft. "Look," he said, pointing upwards. "They sometimes chuck 'em down here."

Dushma hadn't noticed that the alcove in which they were waiting rose high above their heads, tapering like a chimney to a far away circle of daylight. She stood with her head tilted back, trying to hear or smell some trace of the outside world. How long was it since she'd been out in the open air?

A cloud of smoke drifted past her face. Susskin had struck a match and lit his cigarette. He shot her a sideways glance and nudged her conspiratorially. "Hey, don't tell Ibmahuj, will you?"

"Oh, don't be silly. You know perfectly well Ibmahuj wouldn't care."

"Oh yeah? I suppose he gave you that speech about how there aren't any rules. Take you in, did he? Huh. What he means is, there aren't any rules for *him*. *He* does what he likes. You'll see: just wait till we get to St Gotha's. Here, have a drag." He offered her the cigarette.

"No, thank you," said Dushma, a little primly. She moved out of range of his exhalations.

Susskin was unabashed. "Reminds me of me and the lads behind the bike sheds," he said chattily. "When one of us had got some contraband in past the beaks. It was usually fags, but sometimes someone got some whisky miniatures. Or a magazine." He leered at her through the smoke. "And I'm not talking *House and Garden*, know what I mean?"

Dushma shrugged carelessly. "And I suppose you had midnight feasts?" she asked. She had meant to be sarcastic, but it came out sounding slightly awed.

"Midnight *feasts*? That's nothing. We had a midnight rowing trip! We had this massive lake in the grounds, deep as a house in the middle, they told us. That's why it was out of bounds. There was an island with a ruined building. It was a folly, like a temple or something. We sneaked out of the dormitory window and rowed over there one night. Me and Atkinson-Rambler and a couple of the lads. It was excellent. There was this full moon, almost like daylight. So we blacked our hands and faces with burnt cork so they wouldn't show. And we had a secret signal. We hooted like owls so we'd know who was who."

Susskin threw back his head and cupped his hands over his mouth, the cigarette protruding from between two fingers. He let out a long ululation that echoed back at them from the walls of the alcove. "*Who's whoooo...*" it sounded like.

"We picked the lock on the boathouse. Then we wrapped our sweaters round the rowlocks on the boat, so they wouldn't make a noise. We had hot-dogs, sponge cake, Coca-Cola and half a bottle of banana daiquiri that someone'd swiped from their aunt's place."

"It does sound rather exciting," said Dushma grudgingly.

"Well, actually," said Susskin, a remote expression stealing over his face, "actually it was rather weird. The island wasn't as good as it looked from the shore. There was loads of undergrowth, ivy and stuff. And brambles. Nowhere proper to sit down. And by then the novelty was wearing off."

Susskin was frowning and his eyes had an unfocused look, as if long-buried memories were rising to the surface of his mind. "But the funny thing was, after we'd landed, the hooting didn't stop. At first everybody thought it was one of the others, messing around. Then one of the chaps remembered this story about someone who was supposed to have drowned in the lake, years and years before. And this hooting noise went on and on, and we could tell it wasn't one of us."

"Goodness me, let me guess. A *real* owl, maybe?" Dushma had decided Susskin was trying to scare her, and was determined to appear nonchalant. He ignored her.

"Then we heard these splashing sounds. We couldn't tell where they were coming from. It seemed like it was from all around. All of us could swim and it wasn't far to the shore, but someone started going on about the weeds on the bottom of the lake. They wrap themselves around your legs, you see, and pull you down. And then the creepy thing is, eventually, years later, the plant dies. Or the gases in your body make you buoyant enough to pull its roots out. So up you pop, grinning in the moonlight. And then away you go, bobbing across the lake, swollen up like a lilo."

By now Susskin seemed completely unaware of Dushma's presence. He was no longer casting sly glances at her to try and gauge her reaction, but had crouched down and was leaning his chin on his hands, talking almost to himself.

"Who went first? I don't know. The next thing I remember, we're all back in the boat. We hadn't even unpacked the food. Then the sweaters we'd put round the rowlocks got all tangled up with the oars. We couldn't row properly. Someone was shouting that it must be the weeds, dragging us down already. I don't know how we got to the shore. Nobody would look in the water, in case of what they'd see.

"And who shopped us up? I don't know. Could've been anyone. When we got to the dorm we couldn't open the window. We banged on the glass but no one would let us in. They'd locked us out! The frogging bastards locked us out!" Susskin had clenched his hands and screwed up his face in anger; the cigarette smouldered forgotten in one fist.

"Then the moon went in. It was almost completely black. We went round to the front and rang the bell but nobody came. The wind got up and knocked an empty dustbin over. Somebody wet himself. You could smell it.

"They left us out there all night. Then in the morning someone came to get us and we were sent to see the headmaster. Atkinson-Rambler couldn't stop shivering. And laughing. He was laughing all the time. His trousers were soaking. He kept going on about how we'd had to try and save this boy from drowning. At the time the rest of us thought he was trying to be cunning. We all got flogged though, anyway. Before breakfast too."

Susskin remembered his cigarette and took a long pull on the dog end that remained. He choked, coughed rackingly, then gasped for breath and choked again. He staggered to his feet from where he had been crouched and steadied himself against the wall.

"Eeeuch … 'scuse me…" he managed to say, before breaking into another fit of coughing.

"Well, if you will smoke those things…" Dushma was rather glad that something ordinary like this had happened to dispel the sombre mood. She clapped him twice across the back with the palm of her hand.

The effect was extraordinary. He gave a shriek, flung his arms protectively over his head and sprang away from her as if stung.

"Don't you dare… Don't you *dare* touch me!" He looked back at her over the crook of one elbow. His face was crumpled and there were tears on his cheeks, whether from his coughing fit or not Dushma couldn't tell.

"I'm sorry, I didn't mean…" Dushma reached out instinctively towards him and then snatched her hand away again when he flinched.

"What do you care? Frog off, OK? Just *frog off*."

"Oh. All right then, if you're going to be like that…"

A tattoo thrummed along the rail next to them. They heard the sound of footsteps, approaching down the tunnel from the station.

By the time Beltrowser arrived, Susskin was facing the wall and coughing rather artificially into a large white handkerchief.

"Been at the fags again?" asked Beltrowser cheerfully. "Don't tell Ibmahuj, eh?"

"Huh," said Susskin indistinctly. "Fat lot he'd care."

Dushma had been inside St Gotha's Cathedral many times before. When she wanted to escape the crowded streets or

149

the summer heat, she found its huge, dark recesses perfect for losing herself in. She had often spent an afternoon curled up on a pew with a book, or wandering through the many chapels clustered round the nave. She was sure she could spend a whole year in the cathedral and still not have seen every stained-glass tableau or carved marble plaque.

She had never been up any of the towers or down into the crypt, because to do this she needed money and she never had enough. Nor had she ever switched on a votive light beneath the hologram of the saint. Beside the tray of light bulbs was a brass box with a slot in it for coins: it didn't seem worth wasting money on, but she could never quite bring herself to cheat and switch one on without paying.

Even when the cathedral appeared to be empty, she could never feel sure that no one was watching. There were statues everywhere; they stood in niches in the pillars along the nave, reclined on top of sepulchres set into the walls, or perched around the corbels supporting the vast fan-vaulted ceilings. There were also countless gargoyles fashioned from stone, wood or metal in the shape of birds, animals and imaginary creatures. They lurked unexpectedly in corners or peered out of alcoves with jewelled eyes that glittered in the light from the stained-glass windows.

"You know the north transept?" asked Beltrowser. "The one with King David's Chapel in it?"

"Of course," said Dushma.

"Well, we're right beneath it now. This ladder goes up inside the wall."

The tunnel in which the three of them stood was different to the others they had passed through. Instead of being lined with concrete, the walls were made of crumbling brick. In even the gloomiest of the other tunnels there had been occasional electric lights, each just bright enough for them to pick their way until they neared the next one. But here no cables ran overhead, and they had to use torches to guide their footsteps over the uneven flagstones.

They had come to a halt beside a narrow metal ladder. It rose vertically up the side of the tunnel and disappeared into a shaft above their heads. A dull note rang out as Beltrowser tapped his knuckles on one of the rungs.

"Further up it turns into the lightning conductor for the central steeple," he went on. "But don't worry, lightning conductors dissipate charge. So if you climbed this in a storm the worst that would happen is that your hair stood on end."

Dushma reached gingerly for one of the rusty metal uprights of the ladder. If she had been walking across the right sort of carpet she sometimes got an electric shock when she touched a metal rail or a door handle. But now she felt nothing. She tightened her grip on the cold, rough metal, imagining the tip of the lightning conductor trembling in the wind almost two hundred metres above her.

"I've been thinking," said Beltrowser, "if I hooked a big enough capacitor up to this in a thunderstorm I could store a huge amount of electricity."

"For when the revolution comes," snickered Susskin sarcastically.

They ascended in silence but for the occasional squeak of a rubber sole on the ladder. Beltrowser had gone first, and then Susskin. They had hooked their torches to their belts, and at first Dushma's progress was assisted by the illumination from above. But the other two soon outpaced her and she climbed on alone in her own swinging skirt of light.

She tried to count the rungs but soon gave up. Before long she found she needed all her concentration simply to keep moving. A burning pain took root beneath her shoulder blades. Scapula, she told herself. *The shoulder blade is called the scapula.* Surely an ascent such as this was nothing compared to hanging from the iron grating outside the living-room window while Rapplemann's henchmen ransacked her flat.

She stopped to rest, wrapping her elbows round the ladder. Sweat trickled into her eyebrows and made them itch. She pressed her forehead against a rung and moved it from side to side to scratch herself.

A thin needle of cold air touched her cheek and she jumped. Recovering herself, she stretched her neck in the direction of the draught. Not daring to take her hands from the ladder, she tilted her face this way and that. The current of air moved from her ear across her lips to the tip of her nose. Dipping her head, she saw a flash of gold in the wall in front of her.

There was a chink in the masonry just a few centimetres from her eye. So thick was the stone that the light from the other side of the wall was invisible from all but the narrowest of angles. She moved closer but for a moment she couldn't focus. Then she realized that she was looking out into the vast, airy space of the inside of St Gotha's Cathedral. The gold gleam that had attracted her attention was a gilded star on the roof of the nave, shining softly in the glow of a spotlight.

She looked for a long time, rising on tiptoe or bending her knees to alter her angle of view, fascinated by this new perspective on items she knew well. She could see the filigreed pinnacles of the reredos above the high altar, a section of mosaic floor, the topmost lights of a rose window and the hanging chains of dozens of candelabra.

At last she pulled back, blinking, her eyes watering. After days of tunnels and the still air of the underground, the sense of space inside the cathedral left her dizzy with excitement. And she was so high up she must be nearly at the roof by now. Her energy rekindled, she resumed the ascent.

Before long her groping fingers found thin air instead of the next rung. A strong hand grasped her wrist and Beltrowser helped her up on to a narrow wooden platform beneath a sloping roof.

Susskin sat nearby with his back against the wall, drumming his fingers in ostentatious impatience. "Shame no one's fitted a lift, isn't it?" he said.

153

"Oh ... I don't know," panted Dushma. She was determined not to let his bad mood deflate her own exhilaration. "You appreciate the view more if ... if it's difficult to get there."

"Huh."

"You may have a point there," said Beltrowser. "The effort forces more blood into your eyeballs."

From then on the going was less arduous. In the wall next to the top of the ladder was a narrow opening that led to a spiral staircase. There were still no windows, but with her hands free to hold her torch Dushma found it easier to see where she was going.

"We're inside the wall of the central tower," explained Beltrowser from behind her as they climbed. "It can't be the only way up. I think it must be a secret passage, added by the builders for them to hide in if they were persecuted."

After a while Dushma noticed the first faint signs of daylight up ahead of her. Susskin had hurried on, but now she saw him again, heading back down the steps towards her.

"She's here!" he hissed at Beltrowser. "He's brought her. I knew it!"

"Oh go on, don't be silly. She's perfectly all right."

"But she doesn't like me…"

"Rubbish! Well, OK, she was maybe a bit offended when you told that story about Raquel Fairblush getting caned in front of the whole school for dyeing her hair blonde and running off with a boy from the town… But I'm sure she's forgiven and forgotten. I mean, you did apologize."

"Huh. Didn't exactly have much choice, did I?"

A few minutes later Dushma emerged behind the reluctantly slouching Susskin on to the top of the central tower of St Gotha's Cathedral. In front of her was a low parapet. Behind her rose the spiny ribs and scaly shingles of the spire, surmounted by a golden cross that seemed to sway in the darkening sky as she craned her neck to look up at it.

A gentle breeze stirred the escaped strands of hair that straggled across her temples. The evening sun sat a few degrees above the horizon, a flattened, magnified oval glowing an angry pink. Blinking in the light, she staggered as she turned this way and that, trying to take in the whole extraordinary view at once.

A hand at her elbow steadied her. "Welcome!" said a voice in her ear.

Ibmahuj stood next to her, one arm swept out in a proprietorial gesture to indicate the city spread out below them. It was the first time she had seen him other than in semi-darkness. His dark skin gleamed in the sunlight. His beard was shaved to a thin curve from ear lobe to chin, and his eyes were hidden behind metal-rimmed mirror shades. He wore a sleeveless T-shirt that showed off his wiry biceps.

His teeth flashed white in his face. "Glad you could make it," he said. "Come with me. There's someone I'd like you to meet."

Further round the base of the steeple sat a curvaceous girl in pink plastic sunglasses with heart-shaped lenses, her face tilted sideways towards the sunlight. Her peroxided hair was pulled back into two short ponytails and on her feet she wore a pair of roller skates with translucent pink wheels like large boiled sweets. A lollipop bulged in one of her dimpled cheeks.

"Alison…" said Ibmahuj.

The girl jerked her head up, stared for a moment, then uttered a shriek and began to pull herself to her feet.

"Why Dush honey oh my God! This is wonderful, how did you…?" Alison Catfinger staggered across the flagstones towards them, arms outstretched and knees bent awkwardly as she tried to stop her skates running away with her feet.

"I see you already know each other," said Ibmahuj, one eyebrow raised in mild surprise.

"Oh Ibby, me and Dush go way back," exaggerated Alison. She slurped noisily on juice from her lollipop, swallowed and wiped her chin with the back of her hand. "Oops, excuse me…"

Steadying herself on Dushma's shoulder, Alison led her to the parapet. "Come on, let me show you the view, 'ave you ever seen anything so amazing? And then you can tell me everything."

Kneeling at the parapet with Alison's elbow hooked through hers, Dushma felt oddly disappointed. Since her meeting with Susskin and her discovery of Hitler Street, she had several times imagined herself recounting the adventures of her underground life to an astonished and admiring Alison. But now it seemed that Alison knew as much as she did.

"An' there's the car park," Alison was explaining. "You can just see it in the distance, look. That grey lump over there. You remember the skateboard? Wasn't it wild? Dunno if I'd dare go down the up-ramp wearing these!" She stuck out a leg and waggled the skate on the end of it.

Glancing over her shoulder to make sure the others were out of earshot, she moved her head closer to Dushma, gave her a dig in the ribs and whispered, "So then, what do you think? Isn't he dreamy? Isn't he a gravy boat? We met outside a nightclub. You know Apollo V in Hackney?"

Dushma shook her head. *So does that mean you're his squaw now?* she found herself wanting to ask.

"Well anyway, usually I can't get past the door, they say I look too young. But he said he could get me in. He knows some amazing places. You'll never guess where we're going tonight. Dwarf Star at the Ministry! D-Funked and Dogger-L are on the platters. He knows a secret fire escape that comes up in the kitchens. Hey listen, d'you want to come?"

Dushma thought of D-Funked and Dogger-L laid out on giant plates garnished with parsley, and wondered whether it sounded like her sort of thing.

"You should see the guys at some of these places," went on Alison. "They'd go wild for you!"

Now it was Dushma's turn to glance instinctively over her shoulder, to see if Beltrowser was close enough to have heard. "Oh, I couldn't…" she said, suddenly embarrassed in case Alison had noticed. She searched for an excuse she would understand. "I mean, I can't … this is all the clothes I've got."

Alison gave a sympathetic giggle. "Oh Dush, you ain't changed, 'ave you? Maybe next time. We'll get you some glad rags. And how about some of that glitter make-up? They've got strobe lights an' everything, you'd look great. I'll teach you to bop, you'll love it. 'Bout time you 'ad a proper hobby, 'stead of wandering round old churches all the time."

"That's not all I do," said Dushma defensively. "Since I've been at Hitler Street I've learned Ohm's law. And we're going to build a fountain in the ticket hall."

"Since you've been…? Hang on, you don't mean you're *living* down there?" Alison was wide-eyed. "But I thought you said you lived in the viaduct?"

"Oh, that was before," said Dushma airily, rather pleased by Alison's reaction. "You know you said there comes a time when you've just got to let everything go? Well…"

"Hey listen, Dushma, never mind that now." Alison bit her lip and spoke in a rapid whisper. "Are you sure it's safe? I mean, they're like outlaws, know what I mean? Don't you think you'd be better … I mean, you 'ardly know 'em, you never know what might happen…"

"No no, don't worry, they're fine, really they are.

Anyway, being an outlaw —" Dushma shook back her hair — "I don't really have a lot of choice, do I?"

"No, you don't understand." Alison took a deep breath. "Listen, they … I … I mean… Look, don't mention this, right? But I've been in a bit of trouble. You know, for skipping school an' that… My dad dun't know yet, but 'e'd kill me. You don't know 'im. I mean really kill me, you know? But I think I can sort it out, like come to some arrangement… But…"

The clink of glasses came from behind them. "Dinner is served, ladies," said Beltrowser.

"Look, I'll talk to you later, OK?" Alison gave Dushma's arm a squeeze and turned away from the parapet. "Girly talk," she said archly, laying a finger along the side of her nose.

A blanket had been spread out on the flagstones. Laid out on it were the contents of the two rucksacks Susskin and Beltrowser had brought with them. There was French bread, cheese, ham and hummus, several bags of crisps and a small plastic pot of olives. There was also a bottle of wine which Susskin was opening with the corkscrew on his penknife.

"So what do you think of our eyrie?" asked Ibmahuj.

"Mmm, amazing," said Dushma through a mouthful of bread and cheese. "All these spires and carvings and things … you can't even see half of them from ground level."

"Spikes to prang the damned," explained Susskin with

relish. "Our Sunday school teacher told us that on the day of judgment the souls of the condemned would be shovelled out of heaven and impaled on the steeples of all the churches in the land. Murderers, usurers, conjurors... And all the loose women, of course."

"Well, *I'll* be OK then lovies," said Alison Catfinger. "I'll just 'ang on tight." She gave a snort of laughter and waved her wineglass in the air.

"I've never been this far up before. Do you think people can see us?" asked Dushma.

"I doubt it," said Ibmahuj. "It's too high. We'd have to hide if the traffic helicopter came past, I suppose. But anyway, who cares if they saw us? They'd just think it was the gargoyles, come to life."

"Speak for yourself," said Alison with a giggle.

"Or the angels, in your case, of course."

"And the sunset ... it's gorgeous."

"Yes, it's beautiful isn't it," said Beltrowser. "They say the places with the worst air pollution get the best skies in the evening. It's to do with the particles in the atmosphere refracting the light."

"Ah," sighed Susskin. "''Neath the glaze of beauty, oft there lurks the spectre of decay.' Which reminds me, did I ever tell you that story about the time Raquel Fairblush dyed her hair blonde and got locked in the cellar for three days?"

Beltrowser nudged him sharply in the ribs. "Hold on a mo. It's not your turn. Anyway, I'm sure we've heard it. Or something similar."

Dushma was rummaging through her satchel. She took out *Lives and Legends of Historic London* and looked round at her audience. She had thought that Susskin might be obstreperous and had prepared herself for having to face him down. But in fact he now stretched himself out on his side, head propped up on one elbow, and regarded her expectantly.

"You may have heard this story before," Dushma began. "But I thought, seeing as where we are, it might be an appropriate one to tell." She had no need to search for her place: the book fell open at the right page straight away.

"This," she said, "is the story of the martyrdom of St Gotha Angstrom."

VIII

Sir Terence Elkie was a handsome, charming man of graceful manners and an excellent constitution. He was also the richest mill owner in the county. Thousands of workers toiled night and day at his looms, weaving him the cloth that he exported all over the world in his fleet of sturdy merchant vessels. So shrewd a businessman was he that from his humble beginnings as a clerk in his uncle's office, he soon amassed a fortune that was the envy of all but the highest nobles in the land.

Sir Terence owned mansions in the countryside with more rooms than a man could spend time in in twenty years. He had houses on all the fashionable streets in London, fronted with the finest hand-carved marble and frequented by the brightest stars of the capital's society. He kept scores of Arab thoroughbreds to pull his gilded carriages and his walls were hung with portraits by the greatest artists of the time.

Yet as Sir Terence Elkie entered early middle age, he

was not a happy man. His wife, the Lady Meribel, was several years his senior. Her health was not good, and she seldom left her bed. She had borne Sir Terence no children. Though no one who knew Sir Terence would question his devotion to his spouse, it was tacitly acknowledged that their union had been a mutually beneficial one. Through their marriage the acumen and enthusiasm of the young cloth-merchant's clerk was brought to bear on the wide-reaching but failing business interests of Lady Meribel's father. In time the old man's investments were transformed, and on his death became the legacy that was to be the foundation of his son-in-law's great wealth.

But the more success Sir Terence achieved, the less it seemed to interest him. He spent less and less time at parties or out hunting. He even began to leave his business dealings more and more to his agents. His friends tried to draw him into politics – he could afford to reach the top, they told him – but he would have none of it. The only thing that gave him pleasure was his laboratory.

Sir Terence's hobby was magnetism. He had what was rumoured to be the finest collection of magnets in the country, and it had long been his preferred recreation to retire to his laboratory and experiment with them. Over the years, Sir Terence's interest in science had become more than that of a mere dilettante. He read widely on his subject, and had corresponded with some of the most learned figures in the field. His laboratory was fitted out with oak benches and leather-upholstered stools. His brass instruments were fashioned by watchmakers and his glassware came from Venice.

As he grew older, Sir Terence began to spend more and more time at his scientific investigations. He became convinced that he could discover something that would preserve his name as a man of learning. He often worked late into the night, dining alone in his laboratory. It was not unusual for his butler, returning to collect the tray, to find the meal untouched: the meat cold, the gravy congealed and the port decanter still firmly stoppered.

Yet, despite the waning of his interest in commercial matters, Sir Terence did not entirely neglect his business. Although sometimes he would pass days on end without seeing the Lady Meribel, he still found time for regular trips to his mills and factories. It was on one of these visits that a new and unusual employee caught his attention.

She worked at a mechanical loom in one of Sir Terence's cloth mills. She stood out immediately because of her hair, which shone as bright and golden as a candle flame in the gloom of the cavernous weaving room. And unlike the other workers, she did not bow her head when Sir Terence passed along the aisle between the machines, but looked directly at him with a frank and steady gaze.

He had only seen her for an instant, but over the next few weeks Sir Terence found himself returning to that particular mill more often than was strictly necessary. At first he told himself that it would be as good a place as any to begin trying out the new weaving techniques he was thinking of introducing. He even discussed as much with the foreman on one or two occasions. Yet on each visit he found himself taking a particular route across the crowded floor of the weaving room. Each time he managed to catch a surreptitious glimpse of a golden head of hair, and was able by and by to build up a picture of its owner. On one occasion he noticed her fine, almost bone-white complexion; on another, her delicate chin and high, well-defined cheekbones; and on another, her vivid blue eyes and generous, rosy mouth.

Sometimes he saw her close to and sometimes further off, half-hidden by the latticework of threads with which the looms were strung. Once or twice he heard her speak, not with the flat and twangy local accent, but with a merry, sing-song voice that sounded slightly foreign: Scandinavian, perhaps.

Mindful of his reputation, Sir Terence didn't dare to make direct enquiries about the girl's identity. Instead he mentioned to the foreman that his housekeeper was looking for presentable staff, and could he recommend any of the mill workers? There was one person, replied the foreman, a Swedish girl, pious and quite well educated, from a seafaring family that had fallen on hard times. She was a conscientious worker and he would miss her, but he was sure Sir Terence would see him right and he would be happy to send her round for the housekeeper's inspection.

So it was that Gotha Angstrom came to work in the household of Sir Terence Elkie. At first her duties were menial. She helped with the housework, folding linen, fetching water, dusting furniture, polishing silver and assisting where required in the many other duties that were necessary for the orderly running of the household. However it soon became clear that she could be entrusted with more important tasks, and Sir Terence was able to arrange for her to become the maid assigned to his secretarial staff.

This was pleasanter work than making beds and building fires. Gotha's duties now consisted of mixing ink, sharpening quills and cutting the pages of the leather-bound ledgers ready for the clerks to write in them. But she was a quick-witted, literate girl, who soon learned the workings of Sir Terence's filing system. She enjoyed the musty smell of the paper and the acrid tang of the ink, and would often stay behind after the clerks had gone home and tidy up their books and papers for them. Before long the staff of Sir Terence's office began to find that they were more organized than they had ever been. Lost documents and missed deadlines became a thing of the past. They did not guess the real reason for this, and instead congratulated themselves on their improved efficiency.

One evening when all his clerks had left, Sir Terence came looking for someone to write a letter for him. The foreman who had recommended Gotha as a servant had asked that in return Sir Terence furnish him with a reference for a position in London. He was good at his job and Sir Terence didn't want to lose him, but he was a fair employer and did not wish to stand in the way of the foreman's career.

Finding no one but Gotha in his offices, Sir Terence was struck by the thought that the former mill worker probably knew the foreman better than he did. Could she not provide a reference, he joked. To his surprise she took him seriously, and within half an hour sought him out and presented him with the letter she had written.

She had a fine, bold hand, but some of her turns of phrase were a little peculiar. "He is a right hand-man," she had written of the foreman. Sir Terence was delighted. Rather than correcting it, he had the letter dispatched exactly as it was. "Let's see what they make of that, then!" he said to himself.

From then on Sir Terence often made use of Gotha's clerical skills when he needed something written in a hurry out of office hours. He arranged for a desk to be set up for her in the little storeroom off the main office, where the ink was mixed and the least-used ledgers were shelved. He gave her a set of quills to use, and an inkstand and a blotter. He did all this discreetly, so that the other clerks would not be suspicious or resentful of such an unusual situation.

By this time, Sir Terence's work in his laboratory was becoming almost the only thing he did when not managing his business affairs. By now he was seeing the Lady Meribel scarcely more than twice a week. Whenever he tried to talk to her about the progress he was making with his experiments, she would complain of a headache and retire to her chambers. So Sir Terence repaired to his magnets and his chemicals and laboured late into the night.

On one of these evenings it was not Sir Terence's butler but Gotha who came to take away the tray on which his supper had been brought. "Excuse me, sir," she said, standing in the doorway and curtseying low. "Mrs Midgely says that Mr Symes has become someone else and that I should fetch the tray because … because otherwise, it won't be done." She spoke hesitantly and as she did so she stared around the room, her eyes wide.

The laboratory was well lit: apparatus gleamed and glassware glinted in the light of dozens of candles. Some of the brass instruments resembled the sextants and dividers a seaman might use for navigation; others were much more mysterious in their intended purpose. Cabinets lined the walls, filled with bottles containing liquids of many different colours. An easel stood in one corner, holding an intricate map of the constellations. Looking round the room, Gotha was reminded of the ships' chandlers she had visited with her father when she was little. She felt the same excitement as she had then: a feeling of adventure and a sense of mystery and discovery.

"I'm sorry to hear that Mr Symes is not himself," said Sir Terence. Looking up from his experiment he noticed Gotha's curiosity. The frank interest in her gaze reminded him of her expression the first time he had caught sight of her, in the weaving room of the mill. Throwing caution to the winds, he straightened up and said, "Have you never been in a laboratory before? Please, come in and have a look around."

"Why, thank you sir, but I'm sure I should not, Mrs Midgely will be waiting." Gotha moved towards the tray and saw that Sir Terence had not touched his supper. "But sir, you have eaten nothing!" she exclaimed. "Forgive me, I know little of such things, but I have heard that fasting is not good for maintaining a balance of the humours."

It had been a long time since anyone had criticized Sir Terence. Not even Symes the butler would have dared to raise an eyebrow at the fact that his master had not eaten. But rather than annoyance, Sir Terence felt a pang of delight that Gotha should express such guileless concern about his welfare.

"Well, perhaps I shall have a little port before you take the tray away. Which means that you must stay a while, since if the tray returned without its decanter Mrs Midgely would be thrown into utter confusion." He withdrew the stopper and poured himself a splash of the deep purple liquid. Glass in hand, he went to one of the cabinets and took out one of his strongest magnets.

"Watch!" he said. Placing his glass down on a workbench, he held out the magnet in one hand and took a piece of iron between the finger and thumb of the other. For a few seconds he waved the piece of iron slowly in the air like a conjuror. Then abruptly he splayed his fingers. There was a click, and the iron was gone. The hand he held palm outwards towards Gotha was empty.

He laughed good-humouredly at her expression, and handed her the magnet with the piece of iron stuck to one of its faces. "It's a lodestone," he explained, as Gotha tried to prise the iron free.

"Like a compass, that vessels are steering by?" she asked.

"Yes, that's right," replied Sir Terence, somewhat surprised. "Only much more powerful. This is one of my best examples."

He moved towards the workbench where his experiment was set up, and gestured at the apparatus. "It is my ambition to find out the source of this magnetic flux that inhabits some metals but not others. Can it be altered by heating or cooling, or, as I am investigating here, the application of vitriol?"

"Is it not dangerous?" asked Gotha, stepping forward a few paces and looking at the gently smoking liquid in Sir Terence's glass retort.

"Not if one is careful. Though I must confess that when I was less experienced I had some narrow escapes." Sir Terence pointed to a thin white scar on one forearm, just below his rolled-up shirt-sleeve. "I got this when a poor-quality test tube exploded in my hand. Now I buy all my glassware from Venice, where, as you may know, the finest is made."

His glass of port in one hand, Sir Terence picked up the smoking retort with the other and held it up to the light. Immersed in the bubbling acid was an irregularly shaped piece of metal. "Some of the strongest lodestones come from the heavens," explained Sir Terence. "To which the scientific mind immediately responds, is magnetism a characteristic of these fragments of the firmament? Or have they been imbued with it as a result of their descent? I have heard that in France two brothers have constructed a vessel whereby several men may be elevated many thousands of feet above the ground. I intend to write to them and propose an experiment in which pieces of metal are jettisoned from a great height and then examined for any alteration in their magnetic properties."

"You would have to be most careful, sir, that no one was walking about underneath," murmured Gotha.

Sir Terence shot her a keen look to see if she was making fun of him, but her expression was serious and her eyes were round with concern. "Yes, that's true," he replied. "It would have to be done in a sparsely populated area."

"I know little about this," began Gotha after a few moments' silence, "but I have heard that there is much iron and other metal beneath the surface of the earth. Might not their magnetism explain the tendency of objects to fall groundwards?"

Sir Terence opened his mouth to reply and then paused, completely at a loss. This was, as far as he was aware, a totally new line of thought. "Well, I … I don't know…" he began. Then he was struck by the weakness in Gotha's argument. "Aha, but what about paper?" He pulled a crumpled letter from his breeches and waved it about near the magnet. "You see? Utterly indifferent to the lodestone's flux, and yet —" he released the letter and it swooped down on to the bench.

"But it does not always act in such a manner," remarked Gotha. "I have seen paper that's been thrown on the fire blow up and out of the chimney."

"Of course, of course. Magnetic forces are not the only ones at work," murmured Sir Terence, pacing backwards and forwards, one hand to his chin. He could not recall having had a conversation as interesting as this in a long time.

Opening another of his cabinets, he drew forth an opaque, dull orange object. "Amber," he explained. He tore several small pieces from one corner of his letter and piled them in a small heap in the bench in front of Gotha. He rubbed the amber vigorously against his thigh and then held it above the scraps of paper. Several of them twitched as if stirred by a breeze, and one or two sprang up from the bench when Sir Terence lowered his hand.

"A force, you see," he said, "but is it a magnetic one? A magnet does not increase perceptibly in strength when rubbed. The only physical change occasioned in the amber through rubbing is an increase in its temperature."

"And hot air rises!" exclaimed Gotha.

"And yet when the amber is *heated*, it gains no appreciable attractive properties."

Sir Terence handed the amber to Gotha and she held it up to the candlelight, peering fascinatedly into its golden depths. Then she rubbed it on the sleeve of her dress and moved it tentatively towards the pile of paper.

"There, you see?" said Sir Terence, when the scraps rustled and jumped a second time. "Nothing magical about it. In fact, other things work even better. Look at this…" He produced a square of black velvet and a long tortoiseshell comb from his cabinet. After the comb had been drawn just once across the velvet, the whole pile of paper rushed over the bench-top towards it.

"And that's nothing. If you unpin your hair, then you'll really see something." A full-length mirror stood on wheels in one corner. Now, carried away with enthusiasm for his demonstration, Sir Terence moved it away from the wall and tilted it towards Gotha.

"Come on, don't be shy. It'll work much better with you than it will with me." Sir Terence's hair was short and wiry and already streaked with grey. He always took off his wig when in his laboratory, lest it catch fire during the course of an experiment.

Gotha hesitated for a moment before her curiosity overcame her sense of propriety. Shyly she began to remove the pins and clips that held her lustrous golden hair in place.

Sir Terence rubbed the tortoiseshell comb across the velvet until it crackled like newly lit kindling. Then he swept the comb up into the air like a violinist awaiting the downbeat. As the comb approached her head, Gotha's fine hair rose up towards it in a cloud of gilded filaments.

"Ah, it will come off!" she exclaimed. "I feel I am like a

dandelion clock in the wind!" One hand to her mouth, half amused and half apprehensive, she watched her reflection in the mirror. She could see the hair rising and falling on different parts of her head as Sir Terence moved his hand slowly back and forth. The force from the comb felt like invisible fingers running over her scalp, tugging gently at the roots.

"You see?" said Sir Terence triumphantly. "Is there not a strong attractive flux present in the air?"

From then on, Gotha came quite often to collect Sir Terence's tray when he was working late in his laboratory. Sir Terence found himself looking forward more and more to her arrival. In fact he began to find it difficult to concentrate on his experiments, so distracted was he by the anticipation of her presence.

At first they talked mostly about Sir Terence's investigations into the properties of magnets. He eagerly expounded his theories, and gave some more of his favourite demonstrations. For her part, Gotha was fascinated by the laboratory and its equipment. She was quick-witted, and knew something of compasses and navigation from her seafaring father. Her interest was obvious, and she was able to express it through intelligent comments and questions. This made her a gratifying audience and contributed in no small measure to Sir Terence's enjoyment of her company.

She was also able to be of some help with Sir Terence's scientific correspondence. He was engaged in an exchange of letters with a fellow amateur scientist in the United States of America. This scientist had undertaken some ambitious experiments into the electrical nature of storms, and Sir Terence was eager to learn more. He hoped that the American's work might help him in his quest to prove a connection between the attractive properties of magnets and those of amber and tortoiseshell. To this end he dictated several letters to Gotha, who sat on a stool at one of the laboratory benches with her quill pens, her inkpot and a sheaf of Sir Terence's headed stationery.

After this had been going on for some weeks, the two of them felt relaxed enough to discuss more personal matters. Sir Terence learned that in her time off it was Gotha's preference to take long walks across the downs near his house. Finding her not averse to the suggestion, he determined to accompany her on one such excursion.

One afternoon, after instructing his secretary that he was not to be disturbed, he doffed his wig and dressed himself in the oldest clothes he could find in his wardrobe. Completing his outfit with an old, travel-stained coachman's cloak and a battered top hat, he slipped out of a side door in the kitchen garden, convinced that he would pass unrecognized by all but those who knew him well.

Gotha stood waiting for him some way along the path up on to the downs. She was dressed demurely in stout boots and full skirts. Her hair was less severely pinned than when she was at work, and a few golden wisps trailed out from beneath the blue shawl that covered her head. In the crook of one arm she carried a wicker basket covered with a cloth.

They walked for some while in silence, Sir Terence enjoying the fresh breeze and the sound of birdsong. It had been some time since he had walked any distance, his usual means of transport being by carriage from one meeting to the next, or on horseback when he rode with the hunt. He found it a pleasure to be on the move without the rattle and judder of carriage wheels over cobblestones, and to be in the country without the attendant clamour of the hounds and bugles of the hunt.

Sir Terence had given only the vaguest thought as to what explanation he would offer to anyone who saw them and remarked on the unusual fact of their being out in each other's company. Just before leaving, he had taken the hasty precaution of throwing a magnet, a specimen bottle and a quill pen into the capacious pockets of his overcoat. If challenged, he could offer some excuse about being out on a scientific expedition, with Gotha in attendance for clerical purposes. His hobby was well known in the circles in which he moved: such an eccentricity was tolerated and even expected in the very rich.

"We could pretend to be scientists, searching for meteorites," he suggested to Gotha. "Or naturalists, perhaps, collecting specimens."

"Oh, I don't know if I could pretend to be a naturalist," said Gotha worriedly. "You will have to tell me some plants."

176

"But you must know some plants," said Sir Terence.

"I know kirtleweed, rottingbloom and dead man's eyebrows," replied Gotha promptly, her eyes twinkling. "But I am not sure if they are growing this far inland." She caught sight of a cluster of yellow flowers on a nearby slope. "Oh, but those I know," she exclaimed. "We can say we are collecting buttock-ups."

"I think you mean buttercups," said Sir Terence.

"But that is what I said... Did I not? What then are buttock-ups?"

Trying to hide his amusement, Sir Terence did his best to explain. Gotha threw back her head and gave a peal of laughter. "But that is so rude! In that case I will not allow them in my garden. Except perhaps sometimes."

Far from resenting her presumption, Sir Terence found Gotha's teasing delightful. He strode along without a shadow of unease on his mind, enjoying the freedom of the open air and the presence of his companion. He asked about her early life, and she told him about her home in Sweden by the sea, and about cliff-top walks in the sea breeze with the sound of the breakers and the seabirds ringing in her ears. The clear, sing-song quality of her voice evoked for Sir Terence the rise and fall of the waves and the dip and swoop of the gulls. He listened entranced, and then he in his turn told her of his youth as a clerk in the offices of a trading company. Every day, he said, he had recorded the voyages of merchant ships to exotic destinations. He had filled ledgers with descriptions of the routes they took to places such as Jamaica, Molucca and Zanzibar. Later on, ships on similar voyages had made his fortune, yet Sir Terence himself had never even been to sea. It was an ambition of his, he confided. He had heard reliable stories of the extraordinary electrical phenomena that could be witnessed aboard ship. Sober mariners in his employ had come to his house and told of how they had seen the whole ocean aglow with phosphorescence from a miniscule type of sea creature. Others had described the unearthly radiance that sometimes appeared at the masthead to herald stormy weather.

So absorbed was he in their conversation that it wasn't until they reached its outskirts that Sir Terence noticed they had come to a village. It was a small one, consisting of little more than a triangular green surrounded by single-storey cottages of grey stone. Most of the buildings were rundown, having broken windows and slates missing from the roof.

"Where are we?" asked Sir Terence with alarm in his voice. "Are you sure this is wise? I might be recognized."

Before Gotha could reply, a wooden gate on the far side of the green swung open and a raggedly dressed boy stepped out. He seemed about to run forward, then he caught sight of Sir Terence and hesitated. An older girl appeared behind him. Her matted hair obscured her eyes, her nose and knuckles were red and raw and she carried a baby on her hip.

Gotha raised her hand and waved. "Hello Tom, hello

Molly!" she called. "It is quite all right, this is a friend of mine."

It gave Sir Terence an inordinate rush of simple pleasure to hear himself referred to thus. A faint smile came to his lips and he hardly noticed as Gotha removed the covering from her wicker basket to reveal a heap of small loaves of bread. These she began to distribute to the children who now came running towards her across the green.

The boy called Tom was the first to reach her. Barely able to disguise his hunger, he snatched a loaf from Gotha's outstretched hand and bit deeply into it. The fresh-baked crust crumpled under his teeth and flaked down the front of his smock.

"'Ank 'oo kindly ma'am," he said, still chewing.

By the time Gotha had crossed the green her basket was empty. "I'm afraid that's all I have today, children," she said, smiling down at the urchins who still clustered round her skirts.

They had by now reached the last house in the village, and Gotha unlatched the gate and made her way up the short, overgrown garden path. Sir Terence followed cautiously behind her. She knocked, and the door was opened by a hunched old lady whose face creased into a toothless smile when she saw who her visitor was.

"Why ma'am, you're most welcome, to be sure ye are," said the crone, ushering them through into the parlour. "Wasn't sure you'd come again, not after last time."

"And why not? I have said, it was nothing," replied Gotha.

179

"It weren't nothin'. You're a good lady an' 'e 'ad no right." A man sat in a straight-backed chair by the empty fireplace in one corner of the parlour. The room was gloomy and it was impossible to tell how old he was, but his voice was breathless and bubbly with phlegm.

"That's right, 'e 'ad no right, an' 'e'll tell you so 'imself. 'E's a good boy," said the old woman.

"Matthew!" roared the man in the corner, before slumping back in his chair and breaking into a fit of coughing.

An emaciated boy appeared from behind a door, as if he had been waiting there to be summoned. He stood staring at the floor, shuffling his feet and twisting his cap in his hands.

"Matthew, my youngest," explained the old woman to Sir Terence.

"'M sorry ma'am," said the boy to Gotha, bobbing his head awkwardly. "I ... I 'ad no right. To say what I said. 'Bout us 'ceptin' charity an' that. Now I know that pride is a sin, 'an I'm glad for you to 'elp us... Christian charity... Bless 'ee ma'am..." He stuttered to a halt, his head swivelling this way and that, his eyes blinking rapidly. He seemed about to burst into tears.

"If pride is a sin," said Gotha gently, "then I am guilty too, for I am proud and honoured to have this opportunity to help you." With a graceful, spontaneous movement she leaned forward and touched her right index finger to the boy's forehead. He slowly raised his eyes, and when his gaze met hers his face split into a radiant smile.

180

Watching from the shadows, Sir Terence found himself so charmed by this simple gesture of forgiveness that he could not take his eyes from the slender figure standing motionless, arm outstretched, in the centre of the room. He hardly noticed as, leaping backwards, the boy gave a low bow, flourished his cap and sprang out through the parlour door and away down the garden path.

"'E's a good lad," sighed the old woman again, gazing after her son through the still-swinging door.

"So 'e better be or 'e'll feel my leather," muttered the old man.

"And how are you keeping yourself, Mr Walters?" asked Gotha, to break the silence that followed.

"Why champion, thank 'ee ma'am," replied the old man. "That poultice you brung done a world of good."

"I'm glad to hear it," said Gotha. Turning to Sir Terence, she added, "Mr Walters's chest has given trouble to him for a while. I brought him a mustard poultice to help draw out the fusty vapours."

"So, you work for Sir Terence an' all?" asked the old man.

"Mr Jones, at your service," replied Sir Terence, rising a little way from the stool to which Mrs Walters had shown him. "And yes, indeed I do. Have done so for, oh, a good many years now. In a ... ah ... in a personal capacity."

"Oho! Know 'im well then, do ye?"

"As well as anyone, I dare say. But he is a reserved man who —" here he cast a sideways glance at Gotha — "who sometimes finds it difficult to articulate his deepest feelings."

"Deepest feelin's? Dunno as 'e's got none, that 'un."

"I think that's a little harsh…"

"See these 'ands? Bin weavin' all me life an' this is what it's done to 'em." The old man held up his hands, and even in the half-light of the parlour it was clear that they were misshapen. The fingers were twisted and swollen at the knuckles. Their owner seemed unable to straighten them properly. "See that?" he repeated. "Weavin's all they're good for. Can't 'ardly get the top off a bottle no more. But I can't bend 'em right for those new machines, so there's no job for me at the mill. If it weren't for the likes o' Miss Angstrom 'ere we'd be starvin' to death in the gutter and a fat lot Sir Terence would care!"

"Now now, Arthur," said his wife. "Don't you go troublin' Mr Jones like that."

"Troublin' 'im? I can't even offer the man a drink in me own 'ome, the least I can do is give 'im an explanation, can't I?" He waved at a row of cups on the mantelpiece. "You can 'ave water drawn fresh from the well by me own 'ands. It's all they're good for these days, so right welcome you are to it an' all."

Before Mr Walters could lever himself upright, Sir Terence jumped to his feet and reached into an inside pocket of his overcoat for his hip-flask. "Pray don't give it a thought," he said. "I have a little something here, and while my worthiness for such a bestowal is immeasurably below hers, I can only echo Miss Angstrom's sentiments in hoping that you will do me the honour of partaking of a drop with me." He strode to the mantelpiece and began to fill four cups with the contents of his hip-flask, being careful as he did so to keep the monogrammed TE turned in towards his palm.

"Your health," he said, raising his cup to his nose and inhaling the heady smell of the liquor. As he drank, he caught sight of Gotha smiling at him from over the rim of her own cup.

The contents of Sir Terence's hip-flask was the finest vintage Armagnac. He had drunk it from golden goblets in the company of princes, yet it had never tasted richer or more satisfying than it did from that rude wooden vessel in the ill-lit parlour of the weaver's cottage.

"Those poor people," murmured Sir Terence as they walked back across the village green. "I hope they'll be all right."

"I will try and keep a breast for you," promised Gotha solemnly.

Sir Terence hid his smile with the back of his hand. "I think you mean, 'keep me abreast'," he corrected her.

No sooner had Sir Terence returned home than he began to take steps to help the people he had unwittingly impoverished through the technical innovations of his mills. Acting anonymously through his lawyers and agents, he started to plough his vast wealth into charitable deeds. He engaged schoolteachers to educate the children of the surrounding villages; acting under the pseudonym of Mr Jones, he paid several local bakeries to deliver fresh loaves to the disadvantaged of the area; and he revised his bonus scheme to encourage his foremen to take on more new employees.

So involved did he become in these activities that he quite neglected his scientific researches. His favourite pastime was now the regular walks he took in the company of Gotha Angstrom. He would put on his battered old overcoat and hat, steal a cold pie or a ham from the kitchen when no one was looking, and slip through a side door to meet his companion. Then they would set out across the downs together, strolling and talking if it was fine, or, if it was not, striding along together with shoulders hunched against the wind and the rain.

Their walk would always take them to a village, where they would pay a visit to some family that Gotha knew and share with them the provisions they had brought. At first the conditions they encountered were often grim. Yet only a few weeks after his visit to the Walters' house, Sir Terence was secretly delighted to see that his philanthropic policies seemed to be taking effect. More houses had food and drink to offer their visitors, and a fire in the grate when it was cold. There were fewer children with their cheeks hollow from hunger, and more with shoes on their feet. Some of them even clutched books or played with toys.

With each of these walks that he took with Gotha, it seemed to Sir Terence that their intimacy increased. And as this closeness grew, so his caution diminished. He became less concerned about who might see them leaving on their walks together. When they met in the course of their work, Sir Terence would treat her almost as an equal, asking her opinion on matters of business, or entrusting important tasks to her rather than to more senior members of his staff. Normally an astute judge of others, Sir Terence was in this case too blinded by his own new-found happiness to see the resentment that was building among his other clerks.

Nor was it only his clerks who were beginning to feel animosity towards him. The philanthropic working practices that Sir Terence was introducing into his mills were, far from damaging his profits, actually improving the performance of his workforce. But the employees of rival mill owners, jealous of the benefits enjoyed by Sir Terence's weavers, were becoming disgruntled. They worked more slowly and reluctantly, and began to agitate for better conditions. As a result, the quantity and quality of their output declined considerably. Their employers blamed Sir Terence and began to plot among themselves how they could bring him down.

Yet Sir Terence was blissfully unaware of this. He had not been so contented for a long time. His eyes were bright, his step springy, and the fresh air of the downs had brought a healthy glow to his once-pale cheeks. Every minute of the day he wasn't with her he spent looking eagerly forward to his next encounter with Gotha.

He still believed that what he thought of as the friendship between them was a secret from the rest of his household. When he did not see her for a day or two, he put this down to discretion on her part. When she did not appear for one of their usual walks across the downs, however, he began to feel concerned.

The results of his discreet enquiries were not encouraging. His housekeeper, Mrs Midgely, would only say that it was "a bad business", and that Sir Terence should not trouble himself about it. "Good job they took 'er away, that's all I can say. I dunno what for an' I ain't sure I wants to."

Not wanting to arouse suspicion by appearing too concerned, Sir Terence probed no further. Instead he went to his laboratory and paced up and down in an agony of uncertainty for an hour, until a servant arrived to announce that the bishop had called, and awaited Sir Terence's pleasure in the withdrawing room.

"A bad business, Elkie," said the bishop with oleaginous informality. "But I am here to offer spiritual guidance and solace, should you need help in overcoming any lingering malign influence."

"I don't quite follow you," said Sir Terence.

"Atavism is a most pernicious thing," intoned the bishop. "After all, her ignorant ancestors were worshipping Odin and Thor long after our own more civilized forebears had been converted to the one true word."

With a sudden and appalling certainty it dawned on Sir Terence that Gotha had been charged with witchcraft. "Who are her accusers?" he asked, trying to keep his voice dispassionate.

The bishop mentioned several names: some were

members of Sir Terence's own household, and others were prominent figures in the largest mill-owning families in the area. With a twisting feeling in his stomach Sir Terence began to realize how thoroughly he had been outmanoeuvred.

"You must admit the catalogue is damning," said the bishop. "Not only was she seen by independent witnesses, on several different occasions, chanting her vile incantations in your gardens after dark... No, there is not only that, but the matter of the items found in her room, personal items of yours with which she surely sought to strengthen her occult hold over you. Your pens, your ink, a *jacket*... And, beneath the woman's very pillow, a button from one of your waistcoats. Is that not significant? Heaven forbid, for the Lady Meribel's sake as much as for your own, that such things should have got there by means other than felonious ones."

Sir Terence remembered lending Gotha his jacket one particularly blustery day on the downs. It wasn't that he'd forgotten about it, just that it gave him such pleasure to think of it still in her possession that he had never cared to ask for it back. He had not known about the waistcoat button, and learning of it now caused his eyes to swim and his throat to clog with an almost unbearable sensation of simultaneous joy and despair.

It took him several moments to recover himself and bring his mind to bear on the warning implicit in the bishop's words. "I... Yes, no, of course not," he mumbled, momentarily confounded. He was being threatened with a scandal. The trap was even more cunning than he had thought.

"It seems, Elkie, that you have had a narrow escape from the evil intentions of this harpy." The bishop shook his head and composed his face into an expression of concern, but the triumphant glitter in his small, shrewd eyes told a different story.

No sooner had the bishop taken his leave than Sir Terence ordered a carriage made ready. Not even bothering to change out of his walking clothes, he instructed his driver to go to the house of the district magistrate.

"What is this nonsense, Mr Pettigrew?" he demanded, the moment the two of them were alone.

"Damn it all, Sir Terence, a bad business, I agree," replied Mr Pettigrew, delicately applying a pinch of snuff to one slender nostril. "But there are some cast-iron testimonies from people whom it will not be easy to discredit. It's been unheard of for years, but I'm afraid that come the trial I'm going to be left with no alternative but to prescribe the maximum penalty. Unless, of course, someone of impeccable rectitude could be persuaded to give a different explanation for the young lady's behaviour…" He paused and shot Sir Terence a significant look.

Sir Terence rose and paced the room, hands clenched behind his back. "Socially I'd be ruined, of course," he muttered. "I'd have to leave the country…" He stopped in mid-stride and his brow cleared. "So I'd have to leave the country," he repeated with a shrug.

In the grip of wildly conflicting feelings of hope and fear Sir Terence ran from the magistrate's house and, late though it was by now, ordered his coachman to drive to the county gaol. Inside the swaying carriage, he took a small bag from his coat. Opening it, he began counting out the gold he would need for bribes, pausing only to pound the wooden transom that separated him from the driver and shout, "Faster, man!" Sparks flew from the horses' hooves as they struck the flinty cobblestones.

"You have a young lady here named Angstrom," said Sir Terence to the sleepy young gaoler who manned the prison gate. "I would speak with her alone." He held up a sovereign between one finger and thumb.

A suggestive look passed fleetingly across the young gaoler's face. "Oh, yes? And what name should I give ... sir?"

Sir Terence had opened his mouth to give his alias, Mr Jones. But at the last moment the mood of abandonment that gripped him made caution seem pointless. "The name is Elkie, Sir Terence Elkie, and damn your eyes for your insolence, man!" he snarled.

Yet on being shown into Gotha's presence, all Sir Terence's anger and reckless energy evaporated. The cell door rattled shut behind him and he stood speechless, his mouth dry and his heart knocking.

Gotha sat on a low stool, shackled at the wrists. Her dress was torn and dirty, her hair dishevelled. Dark rings encircled her eyes, yet her pale skin seemed more luminous than ever.

At last Sir Terence stepped forward, dropped to one knee and took Gotha's hands in his own. "Gotha ... I'm sorry," he murmured.

Gotha shook her head. "It is my fault, just as much. I should not have been so forward. But I was sure that if you only could see the need those people had, then you would help them. And then I continued with our walks together, because I wanted to help you keep on with the good you were doing."

Sir Terence hardly dared ask his next question. "And was that ... was that the only reason?"

For the first time since he had entered her cell, Gotha raised her head and looked into his eyes. Mutely, she shook her head.

"Gotha, come away with me," said Sir Terence impetuously. "I will speak at the trial, I can save you, I know I can, I have spoken with the magistrate. I know why this has happened. I have enemies, they are trying to hurt me, but my good name means nothing to me now. I would gladly sacrifice my reputation if you consent to come with me once you are free."

Gotha bowed her head again. "I cannot... You know that I cannot," she whispered. "You have a wife ... it is not right."

Sir Terence gripped her hands more tightly and spoke with low urgency. "A noble thought, and I would expect no less of you. But you must understand, my marriage to Meribel is a façade. We ... we have no children. Whatever love there was between us is long extinguished now."

"And is that how she feels?" asked Gotha.

Taken aback, Sir Terence did not immediately reply.

"You know that it is not right," Gotha continued. "I could not live with myself if I made you do this thing."

"And I cannot live without you. So you must choose which one of us you are to ruin!" With a sudden rush of eloquence, Sir Terence at last found words for the feelings that had been building inside him for many months. "Gotha, you have shown me the only chance of fulfilment I have glimpsed in all my adult life. I beg you not to snatch it from me now. In return I promise you your own contentment, and there is surely no virtue in forfeiting that. We will leave the country together, go to America! There is nothing here for either of us now, but to travel, to cross the ocean...! Gotha, please tell me I am not mistaken about the hours of enjoyment we have spent together since first we met. Do not deny that they came to mean as much to you as they always did to me."

Gotha raised her hands awkwardly to try and wipe away a tear from one pale cheek. "It is true," she whispered in a voice close to breaking. "Sir Terence, I ... I am sorry, I..." Before she could say more her face crumpled and her trembling lips twisted uncontrollably downwards. She pulled away from him and, her eyes screwed tight, pressed her forehead hard against her manacled wrists.

Sir Terence remained kneeling for a long time in silence. Finally he rose slowly to his feet and took a step back towards the door of the cell. "Gotha," he whispered, his voice hoarse, "I will come back soon... Please don't leave me..."

She remained turned away from him, her shoulders shaking silently. Sir Terence waited a few seconds more in the vain hope of some sign of encouragement, before rapping on the door to signal he was done.

The days that followed were long and painful for Sir Terence. He kept to his room, or wandered aimlessly on the downs. He avoided his servants, received no visitors and paid no calls. He neglected his affairs and shunned his laboratory.

The day of the assizes drew nearer. Sir Terence tried to speak with Gotha again, but she refused to see him. That night he took a candle and crept up to the garret she had occupied beneath the eaves in the attic of his mansion. The room was entirely bare. Searching desperately for some reminder of her presence, Sir Terence opened and shut the drawers of the bedside table one by one until at the back of the last he found a blue ribbon that he remembered having seen in her hair. Wrapping it tightly around his fingers, he pressed his hand to his heart and stumbled back to his bed.

Sir Terence did not attend the trial of Gotha Angstrom. At the time, he told himself that without Gotha's cooperation, nothing he could say would make any difference, and there was no point in ruining himself for nothing. But when news of the guilty verdict reached him he realized that this had not been true: resentful of her rejection, his motive had been a much baser one. Racked with guilt, he went again to see Pettigrew the magistrate.

"She's innocent, Pettigrew, you must know that," he insisted, a glass of brandy in his trembling hand. "Goddammit, you're an educated man, you can't believe all this witchcraft nonsense. Can't you see, it's a plot concocted to damage and embarrass me. You can't allow this slanderous farrago to claim an innocent life!"

"It's too late, I'm afraid. The time for saying such things has passed," said Pettigrew gently. In truth he was alarmed by the change that had come upon Sir Terence since he had seen him last. Whenever they had met, socially or on business, Sir Terence had struck him as an elegant and fastidious man, but now he was dressed untidily, even shabbily; his eyes were bloodshot and staring and his hair was in disarray. Hoping to calm him down, Pettigrew poured him another glass of brandy.

Sir Terence drank it in one gulp and resumed his pacing. "It's all my fault, you see," he muttered. He stopped and stared into the empty grate. "What a horrible way to die… I keep seeing them all the time, the flames…"

Pettigrew rose and placed a hand on Sir Terence's shoulder. "You must not distress yourself. In fact, I do believe that in these cases suffocation is the most common cause of death, occurring long before the fire has properly taken hold."

Sir Terence shook him off. "No," he said. "There is another way. If you won't let me save her, then at least grant me this." The light of his old enthusiasm flickering dimly in his eyes, he pulled a sheaf of papers from an inside pocket and laid them out on the table top.

"I have long been in correspondence with a learned gentleman in America. His most recent experiments have given me an idea for harnessing the electrical power of the skies." He gestured at a pen and ink sketch on one of his pieces of paper. "For something as crude as this, as you can see, the apparatus is absurdly simple."

"Mmm, I see," said Pettigrew sceptically, peering at the drawing. "I think I get the general drift... But will it work?"

"Oh, you need have no fear as to its efficacy, I assure you."

"But why? It seems ... outlandish."

"Not outlandish, merely progressive. Perhaps one day all civilized executions will be carried out this way. You don't want to be seen as provincial, do you? There would be extra expense involved, I'm sure, which I would be happy to meet..."

Sir Terence stared down at his papers for some moments in silence, his eyes unfocused. "And above all," he said at last, "it will be quick. I don't want her to suffer, you see. It is the season for storms, is it not?"

Over the next few days the posters advertising Gotha's execution began to appear around the town.

"By order of the Right Honourable Mr Lawrence

Pettigrew, Justice of the Peace, it is hereby announced that the foreign heretick GOTHA ANGSTROM, having been tried, found guilty and condemned for Witchcraft, is to be put to death by a New, Ingenious, Humane and Spectacular method devised expressly for this Occasion by noted local personage and gentleman of learning SIR TERENCE ELKIE. Owing to the experimental Nature of this method, the date and time of the Execution will shortly be advised by the Town Crier."

Sir Terence did not witness the death of Gotha Angstrom. Complaining of a fever, he drew the curtains against the humid, threatening afternoon and took to his bed. He lay there pale and trembling, muttering to himself, while the town crier's bell rang through the streets.

He did not see Gotha led through the hastily gathering crowds, a vertical, thirty-foot iron rod lashed to her back. He did not see her taken to the bare heath on the outskirts of town and staked upright beneath the lowering sky. Nor did he see, as the first claps of thunder rolled, the way the mass of excited people surged around her: some struggling to get closer; others, suddenly fearful for their own safety, trying to get further away.

Instead, he pulled the covers up over his head as the sky shivered and cracked with lightning and the rain smacked like pebbles on the windowpanes. With his fingers pressed into his ears to try and shut out the thunder, he recited what fragments of prayers and hymns he could remember. Then he sang songs, chanted numbers, babbled gibberish to himself, anything to keep his mind from dwelling on what he knew must be happening out on the storm-lashed heath.

Hours had passed by the time he finally pushed back the covers and swung his bare feet down on to the floor. The storm had long blown itself out, night had fallen, and a ringing silence sounded in his ears as he crossed the room to his dressing table. With shaking hands, he reached into a hidden compartment at the back of a drawer and removed a small green bottle. Pulling out the stopper, he raised it to his lips.

Then he paused. Although the window was firmly closed, he had felt an icy breeze tug at the hem of his nightgown. He stepped backwards from the dressing table and the bedroom carpet felt wet beneath his bare feet. Raindrops spattered his cheek. He turned, and the bottle slipped from his fingers.

A terrible figure stood at the foot of the bed. Its hair stood up around its head in a blasted halo of frazzled black strands. Its skin was as black and crinkled as charred paper. Its clothes hung from its body in sodden rags.

Sir Terence stood transfixed and speechless. His mouth open and his throat working soundlessly, he stared in horrified recognition as the figure pulled its scorched lips into a smile, its teeth showing startling white in its blistered face.

Then slowly it began to raise its arm towards him.

It wasn't until the following morning that servants found

Sir Terence. He was dead on his back in his bed, his hair perfectly white, his expression deeply tranquil. There was not a mark on his body, save for the sooty print of a woman's forefinger in the middle of his brow.

IX

There were several more paragraphs, describing the miracles wrought by the dead saint's remains, but Dushma felt that this was the best place to stop. She had often read parts of the story aloud to herself, or rather whispered them under her breath. She always finished with Gotha's apparition, imagining herself reciting it to an audience. It still gave her a frisson of fright to read it in bed after dark, or alone in a pew at twilight in some deserted church.

"You can say what you think, if you like," she said after a pause, remembering their rule on uninvited criticism.

"She forgave him," said Susskin. "She touched his forehead like that boy in the village. Isn't that amazing?" There was a faraway look in his eyes and he was shaking his head as if in wonderment. The angry, defiant expression he usually wore had been wiped from his face. His jaw was unclenched and his brow clear.

"Have you never heard that story?" Dushma asked. "I thought everybody knew it."

"Is it true?" Alison wanted to know.

"It's true she was executed by lightning. The rest of it, I suppose it depends whether you want to believe it or not. Some people reckon she still haunts the cathedral, but I've never seen anything."

"Well, I thought it was a really good story. Have they made it into a movie?"

"I don't know," said Dushma. "I haven't seen it, if they have."

"They'd never make a film of it," said Beltrowser cynically. "Not enough sex."

"Oh, I'm sorry," said Dushma in mock concern. "I'll try and remember next time. Although actually, I suppose they could change the plot and have a sequel where their secret love-child goes to America and discovers her special powers."

"It reminds me of when we tied Atkinson-Rambler to the cricket-pitch roller with his braces and left him in the rain," said Susskin. "He was worried that if he got struck by lightning his press-studs would melt and weld him into his waistcoat."

"I really liked the way you did the different voices," said Beltrowser. "Had you been practising?"

"Oh no," said Dushma hastily, looking down at her toes to conceal her pleasure.

"So how come you know that story? Where's it from?" Alison wanted to know.

"I was born on St Gotha's Day," Dushma explained. "I got

this book for my birthday one time. It's full of stories about London. That one's my favourite though. I suppose she's sort of my patron saint. I mean, it's not that I believe all that stuff afterwards, about the miracles and the relics, but I think she was brave and interesting anyway."

"Yaay, she's a feminist icon!" shouted Alison, clapping her hands together. "What did you think, Ibby?" She nudged Ibmahuj with one dimpled elbow.

"I think it was a very subversive story, for its time, about xenophobia and the iniquities of the English class system," said Ibmahuj gravely. He inclined his head towards Dushma. "Thank you for telling it to us."

The sky had grown more overcast as the evening wore on, but now the lower half of the setting sun punctured the clouds like the red-hot blade of a buzz saw. A warm, orangey light filled the air, casting the spiky shadows of the cathedral spires across its sloping roof.

Dushma pulled her knees up under her chin and clasped her arms round her shins. Her veins were pleasantly sluggish from the wine she had drunk with the picnic. She felt that rare feeling of being completely content with the present moment. It came from knowing her time was her own, unconstrained by any imperatives or encumbrances; from being neither too hot nor too cold, not too tired and not too full of unspent energy. Not waiting for something to happen nor longing for something to end; not putting off some unpleasant task nor losing all sense of herself in some enjoyable pursuit, but just happy to be exactly where she was, as if suspended at a point of perfect equilibrium between one activity and the next.

She half closed her eyes and let bright globules of evening sunlight gather in her eyelashes. *If I was a bee*, she thought, *and I was trapped for ever in amber right now, I wouldn't mind.*

Though the interior of the cathedral was almost completely dark, its grandeur did not fail to have its usual effect on Dushma. Even descending the lower reaches of the staircase leading down from the tower, she had felt the fine hairs on her forearms beginning to prickle. When she actually stepped out into the north transept a shiver ran from the nape of her neck down to the base of her spine.

The light from the torches they carried reflected back at them from the polished wood of hundreds of intricately fretworked pews. Bejewelled brass statues gleamed and glittered in their niches in the walls. Shadowy pillars rose up out of the gloom. High above their heads, picked out by the last rays of evening sunlight, gold-painted stars gleamed faintly among the ribs of the fan-vaulted ceiling.

The doors had been locked hours before but still they talked in whispers. Moving cautiously, they picked their way down the nave until they reached a large slab of stone set into the floor. "Here lie the mortal remains of Selwyn Champion Esquire", it said.

Susskin took a T-shaped piece of metal from his rucksack and inserted one end carefully into the deeply carved C of Champion. Twisting the metal key through ninety degrees, he then straddled the slab and pulled. The stone shifted in its setting. There was a low grinding sound as one end of it slowly began to rise. Susskin shuffled backwards and the stone rose further.

Darting forward, Beltrowser wedged one bony shoulder under the raised edge of the slab. He held a thick wooden strut which, as soon as the slab was high enough, he jammed into the gap. Then he pulled a thin coil of rope from his pocket, knotted one end to the wooden strut and threw the other end down into the hole beneath the angled tombstone.

"Careful, don't touch that," he said, pointing at the rope. "It's for later."

Dushma shone her torch into the gap but could see nothing. The slab seemed to rest on top of a thin wedge of blackness. A clammy breeze blew across the floor of the nave.

"Are we going down there?" asked Dushma. "What about the mortal remains of…" She twisted her head to try and make out the writing on the slab.

"I dunno," said Susskin. "I've never seen 'em, have you?"

"Little remains. Of his remains," said Beltrowser.

Susskin was swinging his torch this way and that. "Come on, come on," he muttered. "Where've Ibby and his floozie got to?"

"I think Alison stopped to put her skates back on," said Dushma. "I'll go and look if you like."

Susskin merely clicked his tongue and raised his eyes towards the roof.

Dushma wandered away from the raised slab, shining

her own torch-beam in wide arcs through the deep shadows of the cathedral. There was something Alison had wanted to tell her, she felt sure. If she could find her now, perhaps they could talk for a few seconds, before going their separate ways.

She thought she heard a scraping sound off to one side. "Alison…?" she whispered. But there was no reply, and her flashlight picked out nothing but rows of empty pews.

A shadow stirred at her feet. She jumped before realizing it was her own, cast by a light from behind her.

"Stay near the tunnel," said Beltrowser's voice close behind her. "We don't want you getting lost as well."

"D'you think they're lost? They might just be hiding." Dushma shone her torch along the nearest wall, picking out a row of bronze gargoyles in their alcoves. The way their shadows slid along the stone behind them as she swung the torch made it seem as if they were moving. She had been here hundreds of times before, she told herself. She knew there was nothing to be afraid of.

"Plenty of places for it," said Beltrowser.

"Hmmm…? Places for what?" asked Dushma distractedly.

"For hiding."

They had come to a halt beside one of the cathedral's confessionals. It looked like a tall, varnished wardrobe with two sets of doors, each consisting of a pair of carved wooden grilles. Heavy purple curtains hung down behind these grilles, affording privacy to anyone inside.

"Actually, I think there's somewhere here…" Dushma stepped around the corner of the confessional and peered, frowning, into the empty alcove beyond it. She had hidden there herself once.

"Cosy," said Beltrowser. He was standing behind her, watching her torch-beam sweep up and down the niche she had found. "Only room for one though."

He turned his attention to the confessional. The doors juddered as he opened first one set, then the other.

Dushma held her breath. She found herself expecting to hear the sound of voices from inside the booth. Moving quickly round to the front, she shone her torch in through the open doors to reassure herself that the confessional was indeed empty.

"You know, I've never really looked round here properly," said Beltrowser, swinging the doors shut again. "And there's so much to see. The windows, the statues, the tombstones… And, well, I was wondering … would you fancy coming back some time? Just for a visit. An ordinary one, I mean. I'd really like that. You seem to know it pretty well, you could show me all the interesting bits, tell me the stories…"

At that moment a breathless and giggling Alison appeared from behind a pillar, leading Ibmahuj by the hand.

"Alison…!" hissed Dushma urgently.

"Come on, come *on*! Get a move on will you?" Susskin called impatiently.

Selwyn Champion's tombstone wasn't raised high

enough to make it easy to crawl into the hole underneath. When her turn came, Dushma had to lie face down with her feet towards the hole in the floor. Once in this position she was able to shuffle backwards using her elbows until she could bend her waist around the lip of the hole. Then she felt hands gripping her ankles, guiding her down the final part of the descent.

She found herself in a dry, narrow tunnel running at right angles to the direction of the nave. It stretched away in either direction in a straight line for as far as she could see by the light of her torch. Looking up she could make out the faint outline of the hole left by the raised-up tombstone. The last to descend, Beltrowser was just visible in silhouette against the bluey-grey twilight of the inside of the cathedral.

"Everybody here?" asked Susskin. He stooped and then straightened up again, holding something in his mouth. It was the rope that Beltrowser had tied to the strut propping up the raised tombstone.

Gripping the rope tightly between his bared teeth, Susskin lifted his hands and pressed them to the sides of his head. He bent his knees, crouching down until the rope was taut.

"Better cover your ears," murmured Beltrowser, his lips close to Dushma's cheek.

Eyes closed, Susskin nodded slowly three times, as if counting to himself. Then he twitched his head sharply to one side. The wooden strut came free and the tombstone fell back into place with a boom.

A wave of compressed air squeezed itself down on to their heads. The tunnel shuddered and Dushma felt the vibrations in the bones of her chest. When she uncovered her ears it sounded like the cathedral above her head was still thrumming with the echoes, as if filled with a deep organ note. Much closer she could hear the faint trickle of grit dislodged by the falling stone.

Susskin was holding his torch beneath his chin and grinning like a corpse. The light shining upwards turned his face into a moonscape of bright planes and long shadows. "Every time … a coconut," he whispered gleefully.

The five of them stood awkwardly close for several seconds, each unwilling to move away into the darkness of the tunnel. There was now no sound except for their breathing.

Then Ibmahuj hefted his rucksack on his shoulder, setting the buckles jingling. When he spoke his cheerfulness sounded strangely forced. "We're going now," he said. "We may be some time." He winked at Alison and took her hand, ready to lead her away to Dwarf Star at the Ministry.

"Listen, Dush honey, sure you won't come? I really think you should," said Alison.

"I… Maybe next time."

Alison leaned towards Dushma and squeezed her hand. "Well then, just take care, OK?" she whispered. "Remember, at the end of the day it's every girl for herself, you know?"

For a long time after they had set off in opposite

directions, Dushma could still hear the sound of Alison's roller skates trundling over the flagstones.

They had been walking for several minutes in silence before Susskin burst out, "See? I told you she'd be there. She's no good. She's leading him astray."

"For a confirmed delinquent," observed Beltrowser, "you have a surprising capacity for moral indignation."

"I am the scion of generations of English country gentlemen," said Susskin haughtily. "To me, morels are a sort of mushroom."

Trailing along behind them, Dushma was in the grip of a deep feeling of unease. "You know back there?" she asked. "Was there another way down?"

"Hey yeah, she's right," said Susskin sarcastically. "Why didn't we take the escalator?"

"Not that I know of, but I wouldn't be surprised," said Beltrowser. "The place is riddled with hidey-holes. We can look next time we go, if you like. Why?"

Dushma tipped her head to one side and strained her ears. Was there an occasional, faint scraping to be heard above the noise of their footsteps and the hiss of their breathing? Did it come from behind or in front of them? They were going to think she was frightened. She didn't care: she was frightened.

"No, I didn't mean that... Listen, can anybody hear anything?"

They stopped.

"Hear what?" asked Beltrowser.

"I don't know... A noise, a sort of ... scraping."

"Oooh, it's the ghost of Lawrence Elkie," sneered Susskin. "No more scary bedtime stories for you."

"I can't hear anything," said Beltrowser. "Are you sure?"

"I *thought* I..." Perhaps it had indeed just been her imagination. "I don't know. Maybe..."

"There's a different way we could go, at the next junction," said Beltrowser thoughtfully. "It's more of a long way round, but it's maybe safer. There's no point taking any risks."

"Risk? There isn't any risk," said Susskin. "It's all in her mind. She'll get hysterical next. Smelling salts, ma'am? Loosen your corset?"

"*You* go whichever way you like, and just see if *I* care if anything happens to you," flared Dushma.

At the next junction, instead of bearing straight on, they climbed up to a manhole cover in the ceiling via a set of metal staples in the wall. Susskin came last, muttering sulkily.

The manhole cover led to another tunnel above the one they had just left. This one, however, was much smaller: they had to crawl for several minutes before it opened out and there was room to stand.

"Now we'll know if anyone's following us," whispered Beltrowser.

They waited in silence for a while but heard nothing. They continued on their way and gradually Dushma began to relax again. She no longer glanced nervously over her shoulder every few seconds as she had been doing before they stopped. Her anxiety subsided, to be replaced by exhaustion. Her head drooped, her feet dragged and, bringing up the rear once more, she trudged after Susskin and Beltrowser through the winding tunnels.

X

Dushma had hardly begun to make herself some toast in the kitchen when Beltrowser threw the door open. "Someone's been here," he said.

In the station-master's office a red light was flashing on one of the control panels. The video monitor above it showed a set of horizontal black and white lines scrolling up the screen. Beltrowser slapped the side of the monitor. The lines wobbled for a moment and then continued to scroll.

"Maybe it's just stopped working," suggested Dushma.

There were several old-fashioned video recorders on a shelf below the monitors. Crouching down, Beltrowser selected one of them and pressed the rewind button.

"It's activated by motion," he explained. "So we should be able to see..." He stopped rewinding and pressed the play button. The black and white lines on the monitor disappeared, to be replaced by total blackness.

"Too far..." The tape heads clunked as he punched stop, fast forward and play in rapid succession.

A grainy, black-and-white picture appeared on the video screen. It showed a section of tunnel with a solid, handle-less door set in one wall.

"That's the emergency exit," said Beltrowser. "It's not far from the way we came back today."

Three figures walked into the frame. Because of the angle of the camera it was impossible to see their faces. The leading figure, who wore a hat and a long overcoat, approached the door in the wall and ran his finger down the jamb. Then one of his companions touched his shoulder and leaned towards him as if saying something.

The figure in the hat stepped back from the door, turned round and looked up. For an instant he seemed to stare straight at Dushma. Then he unhooked something from over his forearm and reached up towards the camera. The screen filled with the blurred image of the wicked, forked prong on the curved end of a crowbar. Then the picture vanished.

"My camera," said Beltrowser. "He broke my camera."

He stopped the video recorder and stared at it, frowning to himself. "How much did I have to rewind, from where it was at? Not far at all. They can't have been there that long ago." He rose and turned to leave the room.

"No," said Dushma. "Don't go down there. Please."

Halfway out into the corridor, Beltrowser paused and looked back at her. "That door's solid as the side of a tank," he said, trying to sound confident. "It's fireproof, everything. They'd have to use explosives. Probably bring the tunnel down too." He smiled weakly as he realized what he was saying. "And what else am I going to do? Wait here?"

"Then I'm coming too."

"No…"

"But if it's no use *you* waiting here then why do I…?"

Beltrowser gestured round the station-master's office. "Someone's got to stay here to watch the other cameras. What if they try and get in somewhere else?"

Reluctantly Dushma lowered herself into the high-backed swivel chair in the middle of the room. She didn't ask what exactly she was supposed to do if she saw the three intruders on another of the video screens. She knew it was no good her trying to operate the equipment. Every time she had tried to change channels on their old television at home, the picture had been swamped by static for several minutes afterwards.

When Beltrowser had gone she sat turning the chair from one monitor to the next, staring at the grey, unchanging pictures of corridors, tunnels and doors. She became convinced that at any moment that face was going to loom up at her from another of the screens, just as it had done from the first.

Then it occurred to her that if she sat where she could see the monitors, she couldn't see the door. They could already be in the station. They could already be in the room…

She jumped to her feet and whirled round but there was no one there.

Perhaps it had just been a coincidence. They had been walking along the tunnel, looking for … fare-dodgers, maybe. Or buskers.

She shook her head despairingly. Somewhere in her satchel she still had the ticket she had bought when she first entered the underground. She knew it wouldn't do her any good to show them that.

When Beltrowser returned he found her standing at the half-open door, one eye on the video monitors and the other looking anxiously down the corridor.

"See anything else?" he asked her.

"No." Dushma's shoulders sagged with relief at the sight of him. Perhaps everything was all right after all. "What happened? Have they gone? What's that you've got there?"

Beltrowser was carrying a cardboard box. Entering the station-master's office, he tipped its contents on to the table. A cascade of twisted metal, shattered glass and broken circuit boards spilled out.

"Look at that," he said. "They didn't just break it, they must have stamped up and down on it."

He flopped into the swivel chair and gazed disconsolately at the remains of his camera. "D'you think it was them you heard?" he asked.

"I don't know. If it was them, why didn't they just arrest us in the tunnel?"

Beltrowser shrugged. "To find out where we were going?" He pulled a piece of cloth from his pocket and handed it to Dushma. "Look at that. I found it in the corridor, near where they were."

It was an irregular scrap of lined, grey material about the size of a tea-towel. At first sight it looked like it had been torn from an overcoat, but as Dushma turned it over in her hands she realized that the edges were too cleanly cut. The material hadn't so much been torn as sliced.

"I think someone scared them off," said Beltrowser. "Or something."

"An elidra?"

Beltrowser reached out for the scrap of cloth and held it up to the light, examining it more closely. "Yes, I suppose it might have been," he said slowly. "They're unpredictable. If it was fully charged, and it caught them by surprise..." He looked down again and began raking through the fragments of his camera, trying to salvage bits of circuitry.

"But what are we going to do?"

"I don't know. Nothing much we can do, really. Wait for Ibmahuj, I suppose. I'd go to bed if I were you. Susskin's on guard."

"On guard? Is he safe?"

"He insisted. You should see him. He's dying for them to come back. Anyway, I thought you said you didn't care what happened to him."

"I ... I didn't mean it," Dushma found herself saying defensively. "It's just that he makes fun of me all the time. It's easy for him to say things, he's been to those expensive schools, lived in a sophisticated family..." She knew she was beginning to sound petulant in spite of herself. "What does he want to be so nasty to me for?"

"I don't know. Sometimes it's worse to know you've had everything and thrown it all away."

Dushma felt all her tiredness and loneliness and disappointment welling up inside her, constricting her throat and stinging the insides of her eyes. "No, it isn't! It's worse never to have had anything, and then to think you're finally going to have something, and then to find … and then to find it's all gone wrong…"

Blinking rapidly, she ran to the door and stumbled out into the passage.

Back in her bedroom, Dushma lay down fully clothed in her bunk and stared at the polished boards a few centimetres from her nose. She knew she wasn't going to be able to sleep. Every time she closed her eyes she saw the man in the hat staring out at her from the video screen. Though distorted by the poor quality of the picture, the face had been instantly recognizable.

It couldn't be a coincidence. She was being hunted. First Auntie Megan's flat, then the telephone call, and now this.

At last she got to her feet and peered at herself in the small mirror on the wall. Her eyelids were swollen and there were blotches of grime on her cheeks.

She slipped silently out into the corridor and padded to the bathroom. She filled the sink and stood for a long time with her face above the scalding water, letting the steam clear her nose and listening to the knocking of the pipes.

She didn't know what time it was, but she was sure it was already after midnight. Which meant that today…

Just to be sure, she counted back once more over the days since her arrival at Hitler Street, but she knew she hadn't been underground long enough to lose track of the date. Today was her birthday: St Gotha's Day, public holiday and height of the season of summer storms. As good a day as any.

Returning to her room, she pulled on her shoes and began to gather her belongings. She took her few items of clothing, folded them and put them into her satchel. *Lives and Legends of Historic London* was already in there from earlier that day, and she slid her other books in with it. Then she pinned her hair securely, gathering it up into Auntie Megan's hairslide and fastening the remaining wayward strands with her collection of pins and grips. When she had finished, her pulled-back hair made her face feel taut. In the mirror her eyes looked wider and more awake.

She took one last look around the room. Then she slung her satchel over her shoulder, gripped the leather strap tightly and stepped out into the corridor again, holding her breath as she closed the door softly behind her.

Walking on tiptoe and glancing over her shoulder every few steps, she made her way to Beltrowser's workshop. Reaching the door, she knocked gently and then let herself in without waiting for a reply.

Beltrowser sat at his workbench, a pot of tea steaming at his elbow and a column of smoke rising from the tip of his soldering iron. He jumped when he saw Dushma, and the smoke from the solder shivered in the air.

"I'm going," said Dushma. "I'm going to give myself up. Please don't try to stop me." She had hoped she would seem heroic, but her voice came out sounding small and rather pathetic.

"What? What d'you mean? Why?" Beltrowser half rose to his feet. He appeared more puzzled than upset at her announcement.

"I... It's all my fault. I'm sure it's me they're after."

"What d'you mean? Don't be silly. What makes you say that? Listen, come in and sit down." He pulled a stool out for her from underneath the bench and poured her a cup of tea.

Still holding tightly to her satchel strap, Dushma sat down. Gradually, with much prompting from Beltrowser, she told him everything she'd kept from Ibmahuj about her arrival at Hitler Street. She described the raid on Auntie Megan's flat by Detective Inspector Rapplemann and his two colleagues. She related how she had evaded them and fled down on to the street, and how they had escaped and pursued her, forcing her to take refuge on the underground.

"And then when he phoned up, he told me both the policemen got hurt. He said one of them might be going to die! And it was all my fault because I'd locked the gate and shut them in. And now I'm wanted for manslaughter and that's why they're chasing me."

"Wait a minute, what do you mean, when he phoned up? When who phoned up?"

"He phoned! That time in the car park, it was him!"

"Yes, but who?"

"*Him.* The man on the video screen. The one with the crowbar."

"But why didn't you say, at the time?"

"I thought, if you knew I was a wanted person, you'd think I was a risk to have around. A liability. I thought you might throw me out."

"Dushma, we're *all* wanted. Just because they catch you doesn't mean they're going to stop hunting for us. Now they've found this place they'll go over it with a fine-tooth comb. Then fill it with concrete, as likely as not."

"But they don't know for certain you're here! If I go, give myself up, tell them I was on my own…"

"You've never been in a workhouse, have you?" asked Beltrowser gently.

Dushma shook her head.

"Neither have I, thank God, but I've heard enough stories. Enough to know I'd rather do anything than end up there."

"But what if they catch you?"

"They won't," said Beltrowser grimly. "Don't worry, we've made arrangements."

"But, why? What's so bad about it? Isn't it a bit like

218

school, only stricter? I mean, what happens? Do they bully you?"

"They couldn't. I used to see them sometimes on outings near where I lived. Shuffling along like sleepwalkers. Some people say it's drugs. Others reckon it's something … more permanent. Nobody really knows. Or cares. But there's one thing that is true: did you know once you've been there you can never have children?"

Slowly Dushma let her shoulders sag and her head droop. She picked up her tea and wrapped both hands around the still-warm mug. Then all at once she remembered the photograph she was carrying in her satchel.

"No. When I tell them, it'll be all right," she said with sudden confidence. "They made a mistake, I'm sure they did. With my records. And I can show them." She tilted up her chin and stared defiantly at Beltrowser.

"Are you sure?" he asked gently. "And if you can prove it now, then why not have done it before?"

"I don't know. When I wanted to know why I couldn't go to school, Auntie Megan showed me this."

She undid the buckles on her satchel and slid out the large transparency of the curled-up, unborn baby. Beltrowser took it from her and held it up to the light, peering intently at the vivid purple and orange patches that marked the photograph.

"I don't know what it is," she said. "But I think it must've been a mistake. See those initials in the top-right corner? They're not mine."

"E-E-G," spelled out Beltrowser. "No, they're not anyone's initials. It stands for electroencephalogram. How extraordinary…"

"What's one of those? What's wrong with it?"

"It's a picture of your thoughts before you were born. I've seen other ones, in books, but never one like this before. See here, all this colour round the baby's head…?"

"But how can they see your thoughts?"

"Thoughts are just electricity. And electricity… You can think of it as potential, like water stored behind a dam. Then when that potential gets released it flows as current, and you can make pictures of the magnetic field. But understanding what it signifies … that's a different thing entirely." He looked intently at her with his deep-set blue eyes. "I wonder what on earth you were thinking about."

"But what does it *matter*?" she asked desperately. "How can they victimize you for thoughts you had before you were even born?"

"If a mother chooses to have her baby when the tests show there's something wrong then she's on her own, as far as the state's concerned. Which effectively means that the baby doesn't get registered." He patted his chest. "It's the same sort of thing as happened to me with my heart. If they think you're too bad a risk then they won't invest in you."

"But … I'm not ill. I've never been ill."

Beltrowser held up the photograph again. The colours splashed his face like light through a stained-glass window.

"Maybe it was something the doctors simply didn't understand. You might've been born mad, or in agony. You might've been very expensive. They had no idea what it meant. And for some people, anything they don't understand is a threat."

"If they didn't know what it was, that makes it even more unfair!" protested Dushma. "It could've been their machine not working properly, couldn't it?"

"Well, I suppose it's possible. But I'm afraid you'd have a hard job proving it after all this time. It could've been anything."

Dushma spread her fingers and stared intently down at her hands. "It's true," she admitted slowly, "it's true I'm not good with electrical things. The bulbs in our flat … they often used to blow when I switched them on. Auntie Megan used to get really annoyed. She thought I'd been playing with the lights, flicking them on and off, but I hadn't. Mr Mackenzie – he was our lodger, he said it might be dodgy wiring. But I was the only one it ever used to happen to."

"Was that when you lived in the railway viaduct? There's a lot of current in those lines. Did your mother used to live there? Or perhaps … I don't know, perhaps she was struck by lightning before you were born. Did your aunt ever mention anything like that?"

"I…" She hesitated. "I don't … I'm not sure…"

"Well then, I don't suppose we're ever going to know. So what does it matter?"

"I thought it might've been a mistake," Dushma said in a small voice, her last hope squeezed out of her. "I thought I might be ordinary."

"I'm glad you're not any different to how you are."

"Maybe I could go back to the viaduct…" Dushma stood up, blinking rapidly, and stuffed her photograph blindly back into her satchel. "I was going to cut my hair all off, pretend to be somebody else… Maybe they won't recognize me…"

"Don't do that," said Beltrowser. He stood up and reached out towards her. His long fingers found Auntie Megan's hairslide and undid it. Then he began to loosen her other clips and pins so that her hair fell down about her face.

"You've got beautiful hair," he said. "It's like thick smoke." Picking up a plastic ruler from the workbench, he rubbed it against the sleeve of his woollen sweater until it crackled with static. Then he passed it in an arc over Dushma's head, making her hair billow up in a cloud towards it.

Her throat felt tight and dry. The blood ran hot in her face and roared like a fire in her ears. Before she knew it she had swayed forward and laid her head on Beltrowser's shoulder. His arms came round her and she felt his fingertips run down her spine.

A delicious liquid warmth flowed through her. She felt herself sagging like a melting stick of solder, moulding to his thin but wiry frame. She closed her eyes and rubbed against him, enjoying the luxurious sensation of being able to feel his clothes moving over his skin and his skin sliding over his bones. The sense of panic that had gripped her receded as if sealed off behind a thick glass barrier.

"Come with me. Let's get away from here," he said. When he spoke the vibrations from his chest hummed in her skull.

"Where shall we go?" she asked. Already she could picture the two of them hand in hand on a hillside in the sunlight, her hair blowing free in the wind.

"I don't know. Anywhere. The countryside… Abroad, maybe. I've heard it's easy to stow away on ferries. If you're going out not coming in, that is. Just let me get my things together. I won't need much, just some books, a few tools maybe…"

"No, we can't." For a few moments she had been carried away by his enthusiasm, but now she pulled away from him, her fear and misery crashing back in on her again. "We can't just leave Susskin here. It wouldn't be fair. And what about when Ibmahuj comes back? We have to warn him, let him know it isn't safe here any more."

"Listen." Beltrowser took her hand and spoke intently. "This may be the only chance we get. Susskin can look after himself. And it won't take Ibmahuj long to figure out what's happened. We could … I don't know, leave him a message, or…"

Numbly Dushma shook her head, unable to meet his gaze. "No," she said hoarsely. "You know it isn't right."

Beltrowser nodded and released her hand. "Then … as

223

soon as we get another chance? Tomorrow morning perhaps, as soon as we've talked to the others?"

"Yes," she said. Then she pressed her face back into the hollow of his neck, so he couldn't see in her eyes that she knew that they'd never really had a chance at all.

"Do you promise?" he asked.

"Yes," she said again, her voice muffled. "Yes, of course I do."

"There!" he said happily. "Listen…" He placed her hand over his heart. She could feel it racing. "See? It's stronger already. You're good for me."

XI

"Where are we going?" asked Dushma.

They were walking down the corridor, arms around each other. They went slowly, their steps meandering whenever one of them pressed closer to the other.

"You'll see," said Beltrowser. "There's something I have to show you."

At last he stopped. They had reached what he had told her was the storeroom, the heavy metal door like a submarine hatch in the wall, behind which she hadn't been allowed to see before.

Disengaging himself from Dushma, Beltrowser took a large key from his pocket. He unlocked the door then pulled back on it with all his weight to swing it slowly open. "Tread carefully," he warned her.

The storeroom was lit by a single red bulb and it took Dushma some time to adjust to the gloom. At first it seemed that she was not in a room at all but some kind of cage. The lower part of each wall, from the floor up to chest height, appeared to be made from rows of vertical bars. As she walked over for a better look she stumbled over some bags, solid yet yielding, like sacks of flour.

Reaching the nearest wall, she touched one of the bars and felt polished wood. Moving her hand down she found a chequered grip and a cold, curved tongue of metal.

"Guns," she breathed out loud to herself.

"Muskets," said Beltrowser from somewhere nearby.

As her eyes grew used to the ruddy light, Dushma began to be able to see the old-fashioned workmanship of the weapons racked in front of her. Their stocks were ornate and their dully gleaming metalwork elaborately engraved. She remembered the newspaper article she had seen on the tube train. "The McCulloch Collection," she said.

"Ibmahuj had this idea," said Beltrowser. "We found a shaft going right up into the arms and armour gallery. We took everything, then brought it back in batches through the tunnels, a few weapons at a time. It took us all night. Ibmahuj was sure that before long there'd be lots of us, and he thought we should all be armed. I don't know what was going to happen then, and I'm not sure he did either. Maybe it sounds crazy, but at least it was something to do." He kicked one of the bags at her feet. "We made gunpowder out of fertilizer, sugar and charcoal. Tons of the stuff! Then we cast bullets using lead from the cathedral roof."

He held something out towards her. "Here," he said.

The pistol was as long as her forearm from her elbow to the tip of her middle finger. The barrel was smooth and tapering, the lock and the trigger guard intricately worked. The hammer was in the form of an animal's foreleg, the clawed foot clasping the wedge-shaped flint striker. A chased metal pommel capped the butt.

"It's an eighteenth-century French duelling pistol. A real beauty. Go on, take it. Please. Even if you never use it, I'll feel better knowing you've got it."

Equally repelled and fascinated, Dushma reached out to grasp the weapon. Unprepared for its weight, she nearly dropped it. In films people threw and caught their guns and spun them on one finger. Those tricks would be impossible with a pistol such as this. It took all her strength to hold it at arm's length, and when she did it wobbled so wildly that she could hardly aim it.

Beltrowser showed her how to pour black powder into the muzzle from a measuring cup made of polished horn. Then he rammed a cotton wad down on top of the powder and rolled a round lead bullet in after it. Finally he pressed a second wad firmly home to stop the shot falling out of the barrel.

"This has got a history, this pistol has," he told her as he worked. "Maybe some chevalier used it in an *affaire d'honneur*. Over a game of cards perhaps, or a woman."

He filled the priming pan beneath the hammer with a finer grade of powder. "You draw the hammer back like this until it clicks," he demonstrated. "Then when you pull the trigger, the flint strikes a spark which lights the priming powder. The flame goes through a vent into the breech and

227

ignites the main charge. Hold it tight when you fire it, or it might break your wrist."

But she wouldn't fire it, Dushma told herself. She wouldn't have to, she knew that. She would just point it and people would do as they were told. That was how it worked.

XII

Dushma found it difficult to sleep that night.

She recalled the first real fight she had had with Auntie Megan. She wasn't sure any more what had caused it. It wasn't even the fight itself that made the memory unpleasant: there had been worse ones to come. It was what had happened afterwards.

Dushma idealized the mother she had never known. She liked to imagine what good friends they would have been, how proud her mother would have been of her. It was difficult for her to accept anything that threatened to spoil this fantasy. In the end, however, she had convinced herself that Auntie Megan's bad influence must have been to blame. It had become simply one more item in her secret catalogue of resentment.

Although the reasons for their argument were now vague, she remembered clearly how she had rushed furiously out of the flat, Auntie Megan's hectoring voice echoing after her down the spiral staircase. She had walked the streets for hours, feeling alternately angry and upset.

At last she found herself outside the cathedral. Thinking she could sit down for a while and rest her aching feet, she had slipped quietly inside and made her way to the end of a nearby pew.

Before long she began to feel calmer. She breathed in the smells of incense, dust and furniture polish and was reassured by their familiarity. Distracted by the patterns of coloured sunlight creeping across a nearby wall, she stopped thinking about all the scathing retorts she could have made to Auntie Megan's bullying.

At last she rose and smoothed down her skirt, ready to make her way back to the viaduct. She had hardly begun to walk back towards the cathedral doors when one of them swung open, casting a fan of afternoon light across the floor.

A woman teetered in the doorway for a moment, then began to make her way across the worn stone paving of the cathedral floor. She wore high heels and a sequinned dress which, even in the dim light, Dushma thought she recognized. There was something familiar, too, in the woman's thin-shouldered silhouette and unsteady, sparrow-like gait.

Dushma waited just long enough to be sure of who it was, then backed quickly away into the shadow of a pillar. She did not yet feel ready for another confrontation.

The sound of high heels paused for a moment, then resumed, coming unmistakably closer. Had she been seen?

Trying to keep the pillar between her and the advancing footsteps, she fled further into the cathedral.

Glancing over her shoulder as she went, Dushma nearly ran into the side of the confessional that loomed in her path. She flinched away at the last moment, then felt her way around the carved wooden cubicle and ducked into the deep shadows beyond.

The footsteps had stopped. She could hear the sound of stifled coughing very close at hand. The reek of spirits filled the air, like the smell of sweat on warm metal. She shrank further back into her hiding place and waited for discovery.

Instead she heard the door of the confessional judder open on its rusty hinges. Shoes clunked and scraped against wooden boards as someone stepped awkwardly inside.

"Good af … good afternoon, Father." The voice was hoarse and breathless, but Dushma could hear it quite clearly through the thin walls of the confessional. The priest's reply was much less distinct, no more than a vibration in the wooden panelling.

"No, I'm afraid I haven't been for ages, Father," went on Auntie Megan, after clearing her throat laboriously. "In fact I've never been particularly devout. I've just come for a bit of moral support, to tell you the truth. If I bottle it up any more I'll explode, I'm sure."

Crouched in her alcove, Dushma hesitated. After a brief struggle, her curiosity overcame her common sense and she stayed where she was.

"She'd stretch the patience of a saint, believe me," Auntie Megan was saying. "I try to give her a bit of advice, pass on the fruits of my hard-won experience, but I might as well be talking gibberish for all the attention she pays. She should know what's good for her! How else is she ever going to be able to make a contribution? Is it too much to expect? A little in return for all the time and effort I've invested in the girl?"

Dushma heard the sounds of Auntie Megan shifting uncomfortably and loudly blowing her nose. Then the priest spoke again.

"Of course not, Father!" Auntie Megan sounded aggrieved. "I've hardly ever so much as raised my voice to her. And it's not as if I don't get enough provocation. It's the least I'm entitled to, isn't it Father, a bit of respect from the child I've brought up as if she was my own?"

The priest murmured something in response.

"Yes, sometimes it's difficult to cope." Auntie Megan was now using the wheedling voice that meant she wanted something. "She's very demanding, you see. I was going to ask, d'you know anyone who might… A loan, say, no questions asked, you know what I mean…? The Sisters of what…? Er, yes, that would be helpful, thank you, I'll bear it in mind."

Throughout this exchange, Dushma had felt a growing sense of outrage at hearing herself so blatantly slandered. Now she was tempted to leap to her feet, throw open the door of the confessional and denounce Auntie Megan's hypocrisy. But what she heard next, with its promise of revelation, made her change her mind.

"No, that's right, she's not even mine!" Auntie Megan had seized at her chance for self-justification, and her tone was now pitched to suggest long-suffering virtue. "You know how it is, it was a long time ago. I was much much younger, hardly more than a girl, I suppose you could say. I'd met someone at this camp, or protest thing it was supposed to be, but we were just there for the fun, 'cept she wasn't careful enough and got herself ... compromised, know what I mean? Now I know you won't approve of this, but we thought at the time it'd be better if she didn't have it, see? So I said I'd help her. I thought it was for the best, for her, honestly I did Father. It was something I'd heard from a friend of a friend, just a pair of crocodile clips and a motorcycle battery. But it didn't work, and she was too frightened to try any more after that. So I cared for her as best I could, though it did no good, she died you see, but then I took the brat in, didn't I? Looked after her like she was me own I did, and she's been a trial to me, Father, believe me, an ungrateful, headstrong, wilful child from the moment she could walk and talk but oh no I'm not bitter 'cos I know I've got no right to hope for anything more and whatever I get is nothing but my just deserts so help me God!"

Auntie Megan had been speaking faster and faster, her voice growing more and more breathless as she tried to say everything she wanted to before she gave in to her cough.

No sooner had she finished her speech than a bout of dry and painful retching overcame her, taking several seconds to subside.

The priest murmured something unintelligible, presumably words of absolution.

"Thank you Father... A load off my mind... Yes, bless you too Father..."

From inside the confessional came the sounds of Auntie Megan scrambling to her feet. The door creaked open, then shut again.

For a long time after the clatter of high heels had died away, Dushma had stayed crouched in the alcove, hugging her knees and staring unseeingly at the floor.

XIII

They gathered in the kitchen very early next morning. Neither of the others had been able to sleep much either. They ate the last of their breakfast cereal, though none of them had much appetite. In the bottom of the box was a grey plastic figurine, a character from a children's television series. Susskin ripped it from its cellophane packet and began idly pricking at it with the point of a carving knife.

Dushma was eating with a wooden spoon, because she had found to her unease that the metal cutlery was beginning to stick to her fingers as if covered with an invisible film of glue. At last she laid the spoon down, her breakfast still almost untouched.

"We thought…" she began tentatively, "we thought we might try and escape. Get out of London. Leave the country on a ferry maybe…" She glanced at Beltrowser but he looked away, his face pale and pinched. "But we didn't want to go without warning Ibmahuj. But we don't know where he is. We thought he'd be back by now."

Susskin too refused to meet her gaze. He continued to toy with the carving knife, his eyes red-rimmed from his night spent on guard inside the emergency exit.

Beltrowser cleared his throat. "It's too late to worry about Ibmahuj now," he said. He tossed a scrunched-up piece of material on to the table. It was the sliced-off corner of overcoat he had found in the tunnel the night before. He smoothed it out, reached into the pocket and removed a rectangle of paper. "Never thought to look last night," he said. He unfolded the piece of paper and pushed it towards Dushma.

"Statement of cooperation," she read. "I the undersigned do without prejudice furnish and provide the following information regarding other miscreants and/or misdemeanours known to me. I understand that by so doing I will mitigate those charges relating to me in respect of these or other misdemeanours…"

She skimmed quickly to the bottom of the document and the signature. "A Catfinger", it said, in fat, childish letters.

"Alison! They must have caught her!" she exclaimed without thinking.

"No time. We'd seen her less than half an hour before I picked this up. That last time she was with us … she'd already done it."

Dushma shook her head numbly. Beltrowser picked up the piece of paper again and folded it with exaggerated care.

"Your girlfriend shopped us up," he said grimly. "She sold us out. And whatever she got for us, I hope it doesn't do her any good at all."

"I'm sorry," mumbled Dushma. "I didn't know…" But of course. That was what Alison had been trying to tell her, out of some residue of friendship, decency or guilt. Why hadn't she realized? Would it have made any difference if she had? Would the others have believed her? She glanced apprehensively at Susskin, but he was ominously silent. He had picked up the cereal-packet figurine by its base and was whittling at it with short, savage strokes of the carving knife. Curly shavings of plastic skittered across the table.

"I knew it was too good to last," muttered Beltrowser.

"Oh, really?" asked Susskin sarcastically. "Which bits were too good, exactly? I think I must've missed those."

"What are we going to do?" Dushma wanted to know.

"It's very simple," said Susskin. "You have two choices. You can stay here. Or you can run away."

"The place is probably surrounded already," said Beltrowser fatalistically. He stood up abruptly and fixed his gaze on Dushma. "So I think we've probably had it. That is, those of us who haven't been clever enough to make some special arrangement."

Dushma caught up with Beltrowser halfway down the corridor. "Listen … you're wrong, it was nothing to do with me. I really didn't know, how could I have?"

"Even if you didn't, you still knew *her*, didn't you? Couldn't you have warned us? Told us not to trust her?"

"I didn't know her that well. I've never really known anyone that well. And anyway, Susskin warned you, didn't he? Why didn't you listen to him?"

Beltrowser gave her a pitying look and strode on without replying. Dushma broke into a stumbling trot to try and keep up with him. "Wait a minute ... you can't believe... Look, if they'd got me to sign one of those statements, why would they need to get one from Alison too?"

They had reached the door to Beltrowser's workshop. Inside it was unusually tidy, and a rucksack stood ready packed on top of the workbench. After a cursory last look round, Beltrowser swung the rucksack up on to his back. He busied himself with minute adjustments of the straps, not meeting Dushma's eye.

"Listen... Last night –" her voice cracked – "I said I was going to go, because I thought it might be my fault, and then you said not to, and..."

"Well, you might as well have done, mightn't you?" retorted Beltrowser. "You couldn't have done much more harm than your friend already has."

Dushma felt too wretched even to be angry. "You don't mean that," she whispered. "Please say you don't mean it."

Beltrowser pushed his way out into the corridor and turned to face her. "I don't know," he said miserably. "I'm not sure about anything any more. I don't know how many more coincidences I'm going to be expected to believe in. All I know is, I'm leaving now. You can do whatever you like. I don't care."

"Wait for me, please," she called after him.

He didn't turn or answer.

By the time Dushma returned from her room, Beltrowser was nowhere to be seen. Weighed down with the loaded pistol, her satchel bumped awkwardly against her bony hip as she hurried along the corridor towards the kitchen.

Passing the open door, she paused and glanced in. Susskin didn't appear to have moved. He still sat at the kitchen table, the carving knife in one hand, his eyes staring unfocusedly into space.

"I know you don't want me to come with you," he said before she could speak. "Well, that's OK, 'cos I wouldn't come with you if you begged me to. Just don't count on coming back, that's all, 'cos if they find me there won't be anywhere worth coming back to. There's enough gunpowder here for me to be able to make sure of that."

"I'm sorry. Look after yourself," said Dushma.

"Like you care," sneered Susskin.

Dushma ran down staircases and through flapping swing doors towards the emergency exit, her feet ringing on the concrete floor. She couldn't remember the way, but from time to time a sprinting green stick-man drawn on a sign on the wall showed the direction she should take.

By the time she reached the long corridor leading to the exit her breathing was ragged and her chest ached. She had to stop and lean against the wall to recover herself.

Some way in front of her, Beltrowser was walking slowly towards the twin steel doors at the far end of the corridor. As she watched, he glanced back over his shoulder, anxiously it seemed to her.

"Wait..." she gasped.

When he saw her he turned and his face broke into a smile. He raised his hand and took a step towards her.

Tears pricked the corners of her eyes. She smiled too, so widely it almost hurt. A sob of laughter and relief welled up in her throat. Everything suddenly seemed brighter and more in focus.

Then something behind him caught her eye and her face froze. The doors of the emergency exit didn't look quite right. There was something about them that was inconsistent with the low level of lighting in the corridor. She stared at them hard, eyes screwed up as if trying to fathom an optical illusion.

That was it. The lintel cast its shadow *upwards*, not downwards ... and the ceiling above it gleamed with a faint reflection, as if a powerful beam of light was shining through a crack from the other side.

"*Beltrowser!*" she shrieked.

The double doors flapped inwards before a roiling tide of thick white smoke. A shock wave knocked Dushma to the floor and a burst of noise stunned her as if she'd been clapped over the ears.

Then she was crawling forwards on hands and knees across a pile of shattered plaster and broken laths. Grit crunched between her teeth. Her hair straggled down over her eyes and stuck to her face and her head sang. Dust hung in the air all around her.

A pair of floodlights shone down the corridor from where the doors had been, half blinding her with their brightness. The lights on the walls had been smashed and the bare wires fizzled in their sockets. She lurched to her feet and squinted into the glare. Large sections of the ceiling had come down and the corridor was carpeted with rubble. Nothing moved among the debris.

"Stay where you are!" someone shouted. Though the voice was amplified she recognized it instantly.

"No no no no no…" She was muttering under her breath without realizing it. Lowering herself slowly into a crouch she began casting about for her satchel, snatched from her by the blast.

She heard crunching footsteps coming towards her from the other end of the corridor. Looking up, she saw an advancing figure silhouetted against the floodlights.

Her hand touched the broken strap of her satchel. She pulled it to her and scrabbled at the fastenings.

The figure was closer. She could now see that it wore a hat and an overcoat.

"See what happens when you try to lock me out?" asked

Detective Inspector Rapplemann. "It's not very nice of you, is it? To put us to so much trouble when we're only trying to help you."

Backing slowly away from him, Dushma reached inside her satchel. The duelling pistol seemed almost to push itself into her grasp. Seizing the cold metal pommel she drew it free and threw the satchel down.

Her vision was blurred and she wiped the back of her hand across her watering eyes. She raised the pistol in a trembling grip. The muzzle wavered uncontrollably. She wanted to tell him to get back, to leave her alone and go away, but her throat was clogged with dust and she could only croak.

"I'm sure you've heard lots of stories," said Detective Inspector Rapplemann. "But they get me so wrong, you know? I really like young people. It's true. I really, really like them."

If this was a film, thought Dushma, this would be where he told her that he was her father. She shuddered and pulled the trigger.

She felt as if she'd tried to stop a slamming door with her outstretched hands. The recoil jarred her arms in their sockets. Her ears rang and her palms stung. She staggered backwards, lost her balance and fell.

By the time she had pulled herself upright, she was almost completely enveloped in smoke. Several small fires were now burning up and down the corridor and she waved her hand to try and clear the air in front of her. The smell of gunpowder caught in her nostrils.

She took several cautious steps forward and strained her eyes, but she could see nothing moving in the dense black clouds. She hesitated for a moment, then jumped back as what sounded like another large chunk of ceiling crashed to the floor.

The empty pistol dangling forgotten in one hand, she turned and stumbled back the way she had come. "I'm sorry, I'm sorry," she whispered as she went.

Dushma ran through the station, turning corners at random, a cloud of sparks trailing behind her. However fast she went she seemed unable to escape the heat at her back and the choking fumes in her nostrils. It wasn't until a tongue of flame reached her scalp that she realized she was on fire.

She screamed and beat at her head with the palm of her left hand. Several clumps of charred hair came away in her fingers and she gagged on the acrid smell.

She had tried to throw the pistol down but it was stuck in her clenched right fist. When the flames in her hair were out she tried again to prise the weapon free, but she couldn't unclasp the fingers of her right hand from around the butt. The engraved metal inlays were stuck to her flesh as if to a magnet.

It must be just a muscle spasm, she told herself, clawing at the pistol with the blistered fingers of her left hand. If she could just relax then her grip would loosen.

In the meantime she found she no longer had the strength

to hold the pistol properly. If she let her arm hang loose the barrel banged against her knees, so she had to fold her arms across her chest and cradle the weapon in the crook of her left arm.

She continued her progress in this awkward attitude, walking now instead of running. She stopped every few minutes to listen for sounds of pursuit but heard nothing.

Now that the initial panic of her flight had faded, the image of the burning corridor began creeping back into her mind. During one of her brief rests, sitting with her head bowed and her back against the wall, she was pierced by a sudden jab of misery and anger. Flailing out blindly, she dashed the muzzle of the pistol against the floor. The impact hurt her wrist but did not loosen her grip on the weapon.

She gasped for breath, her eyes screwed tight and her shoulders heaving. It was several minutes before she could control herself enough to press on.

At last, more by accident than design, she reached the platform, the place of her first entry into Hitler Street. Here she stopped for a few minutes in order to make a sling for the pistol out of her scarf. It was difficult to do, but she managed to tie a clumsy reef knot and pull it tight by holding one end of the scarf between her teeth.

She now had one hand free, making it easier for her to lower herself down from the edge of the platform on to the track. Taking care to avoid stumbling on to the live rail, she set off down the tunnel.

The map that Ibmahuj had given her was still in her

satchel, so she had to find her way from memory. It was in her mind to make for the cathedral, but she had no clear idea what she would do once she got there.

She reached the alcove where Susskin had smoked his furtive cigarette. She paused and looked upwards at the opening far above her head. It was still early and she could make out only the faintest patch of light. A distant rumble reached her ears and the fine hairs on her forearms began to prickle. *There's going to be a storm*, she thought.

She left the railway track as soon as she could, pulling herself up a metal ladder into an access passage overhead. Climbing was difficult. The muzzle of the pistol banged against her chest and she grazed her elbow on the wall trying to keep her balance. Slivers of rust from the corroding rungs stuck to her palm.

Reaching the top of the ladder she trod on the hem of her skirt and nearly fell. She was about to rip the trailing section of material free when an idea struck her. She pulled at one of the dangling threads to loosen it further. Having teased out enough to make a good knot, she leaned precariously out over the ladder and managed, one-handed, to tie the thread to the topmost rung. Then she set off down the passage, the thread unravelling behind her.

She soon lost her bearings completely as the passage zigzagged this way and that. It didn't matter, she told herself. She could always retrace her steps by simply rewinding her thread.

She took several turnings at random and before long was

245

hopelessly lost. Around every corner the view was the same: poorly lit, parallel concrete walls stretching away into the murky distance. Eventually, for all she knew, she could have been heading in completely the opposite direction to the one she had started out in.

At last the floor began to tilt upwards. She quickened her pace, her skirt pulled tight across her knees by its unravelling thread. The air was getting fresher, she was sure. Turning a sharp corner, she found herself back on the railway track again.

The section of tunnel into which she emerged was large and well ventilated, the rails polished from regular use. The lights on the walls were of modern design and a gentle breeze ruffled her hair.

Although she still had no idea where she was, at first she was just relieved that she hadn't come full circle, back to the line that led to Hitler Street. Then it occurred to her that it might be late enough for trains to be running. Forgetfully she glanced at her watch, but it was behaving even more peculiarly than usual. The whole display was a-shiver with a mad Tetris game of liquid crystal rectangles.

She looked speculatively at the rails. Would there be enough clearance for her to lie down between the sleepers while a train passed harmlessly above her? No, she decided, it wasn't worth the risk. How was she to know what hooks might dangle underneath the carriages to snag her clothes or hair and drag her bumping and broken like a doll over the sleepers? Besides, she was sure this wasn't the right way to the cathedral.

She turned and gathered up the slack in the thread trailing from her skirt, ready to retrace her steps.

No sooner had she pulled the thread taut than it jerked as if seized by an invisible hand. Her arm was wrenched forward and the thread sliced the flesh of her palm.

With a gasp she snatched her hand away. The thread hung loosely for a moment, then three more tugs billowed her skirt around her legs. Someone had found the other end and was pulling on it.

With the disgusted, panicky movements of someone trying to rid themselves of crawling insects, she grabbed at the thread, put it to her mouth and bit it in two. The severed end twitched in the air, then slithered and coiled its way out of sight, back down the passage from which Dushma had come.

She didn't dare follow it now. She spun round again and set off down the railway line, her numb right arm throbbing against her chest as she jumped from one concrete sleeper to the next. The thread had cut her lip and it stung as she sucked in the chilly tunnel air with quick, shallow breaths.

Someone was catching up with her. Now she could hear their footsteps even above the hiss of her own panting. The soles of their shoes scraped against the floor of the tunnel like the sound of scissors opening and closing.

The tunnel curved and the light grew worse. She could no longer be sure where she was putting her feet, and she had to slow down or risk falling. Looking over her shoulder, she saw torchlight dancing on the tunnel wall behind her. The fine hairs on her forearms prickled like iron filings under a magnet.

Her shin cracked against something unseen and she fell heavily. Her vision filled with jittery streaks of colour like a long-exposure photograph of somebody waving a firework. She lay still for several seconds, the breath squeezed out of her lungs and all feeling knocked from her body.

When sensation returned to her jolted nerves she felt a curved metal surface beneath her cheek. She tried to raise her head but the metal was sticky, making it difficult for her to move.

With an effort she tilted her face and peered upwards.

Above her in the semi-darkness she could just make out a pair of drooping eyelids and a sagging, toothy jaw. Then there was a sound of whirring motors and the eyelids flickered open. Blinking rapidly to try and clear her vision, Dushma found herself staring straight into the dull blue eyes of an elidra.

She had tripped on its coiled tail and fallen against its scaly metal flank. Now she lay awkwardly, her right arm underneath her and the muzzle of the pistol pressing against her collarbone.

Bracing herself with her free hand she pushed herself away from the elidra's body. Upright again, she felt as if a strong wind was buffeting at her back. She had to brace herself to avoid falling headlong a second time. Her skin was tingling from head to foot. The shivers running up and down her spine were so intense that her back arched.

The elidra lay along one of the rails, one flank pressed up against the wall of the tunnel, its wings furled across its back. Its energy was clearly spent. Its head swayed unsteadily on the end of its spiny neck. When its eyes could be seen, their light varied from an almost imperceptible blue to a faint and sickly green.

Dushma reached out towards it with her good hand. When her fingers were close to the elidra's body she felt herself pulled helplessly towards it like a magnet towards a sheet of iron. Such was the force that her palm slapped painfully against the metal.

She remembered setting light to her blouse and the way the electric iron had shone like a stained-glass window from the heat. She closed her eyes and pictured the photograph of herself curled up inside her mother's womb. She thought of the electric trains hurtling over the viaduct, a few metres above her bed, many times every day and night for all the years she had lived there. She squeezed her eyes more tightly shut and saw the orange and purple thought-patterns of her unborn self swirling behind her eyelids. Her ears hummed with the twang and sizzle that had filled her viaduct bedroom every time a train approached.

She crouched and pressed her cheek to the elidra's body again. She began to slide her hand back and forth along its flank, stroking the cool metal scales. A roaring filled her head like the sound of static from an out-of-tune TV set.

"Help me," she whispered to the elidra. "You have to help me. Please wake up and help me."

Someone seized her by the shoulder and spun her roughly around. Her neck snapped back and her head banged against the side of the elidra.

Detective Inspector Rapplemann stood before her, his crowbar slung over his forearm. The lenses of his spectacles glittered in the light of the torch he carried. His lips were pulled back from his teeth and he was breathing heavily.

All the strength went out of Dushma and she slumped like a puppet with its strings cut. Weakly she tried to pull the pistol free of its makeshift sling round her neck. She could threaten him with it, she thought, or try and club him with the butt. Instead she found that her numb right arm would not obey her properly. It flopped to her side, while the pistol came suddenly unstuck from the palm of her hand and fell to the ground with a clatter.

Rapplemann jumped back from her at the noise, then smiled when he saw the pistol lying on the tunnel floor. Dushma noticed that there was a rent in one sleeve of his overcoat. A dark stain covered his upper arm.

"What would you say?" he asked her gently. "*I think I could easily be forgiven for treating you as ... highly dangerous.*" He raised his crowbar and stepped towards her.

Dushma felt a sudden heat between her shoulder blades from the body of the elidra. She heard cogs grinding and gears meshing inside it. It surged to its feet, throwing her forward on to her knees. Raising one cruelly taloned foreleg it clenched at the air with claws like carving knives. Then it struck like a snake, snatching the crowbar from Rapplemann's grasp and twisting it like a paper clip.

Mouth agape, it ducked its long rippling neck. Seizing the crowbar in its terrible jaws, it wrenched off the end with a single twitch of its magnificent head. Its eyes blazed scarlet and a roaring sound rose up from deep within its gullet. It opened its mouth and strands of molten metal dripped from between its red-hot teeth and splashed hissing to the floor.

Springing backwards several paces, Rapplemann reached inside his overcoat and drew out an automatic pistol. His hand perfectly steady, he aimed it into Dushma's face.

"Call it off," he said.

I can't, I can't, thought Dushma. *I don't know what I've done.*

"Call it off, I said!" snarled Rapplemann.

With the hollow slap of a sail catching the wind, the elidra swept open the overlapping foil panels of one of its wings. A great gust of air went rushing down the tunnel. Caught off balance, Rapplemann staggered, stepped backwards to try and recover himself, and trod on the electrified rail.

There was a noise like the crack of a whip and Rapplemann grunted as if he'd been punched in the stomach. Limbs splayed, he was thrown high into the air by the shock. His shoulders hit the curved roof and he dropped down on to the rail again, this time to be flung outwards on to his back in the middle of the tunnel.

251

His arms and legs twitched once or twice and then he lay still, apart from one hand which clenched and unclenched spasmodically for several seconds. Wisps of smoke coiled out from underneath his collar. The smell of charred meat hung in the air. Still on her hands and knees, Dushma threw up.

Wiping strands of phlegm from her chin, she rose unsteadily to her feet. Bile burned in her throat. She felt as if the very floor of the tunnel was trembling beneath her. At first she thought she must be suffering an attack of dizziness, but then she became aware of a faint but regular metallic sound like a ricochet emanating from the rails. There was a train coming.

She looked desperately around her for an alcove in which she could hide, or a ladder or hatchway that might offer some means of escape, but there was nothing.

She turned back to the elidra. It blocked the tunnel, rearing up like a heraldic beast on some fantastic coat of arms. Its head rose and dipped, the links of its long articulated neck purring like a running chain. Its eyes glowing almost too brightly to look at, it stretched and furled its opalescent wings as if newly awakened from sleep.

Something on the floor caught its attention. It struck at Rapplemann's fallen pistol and raised it curiously in one upturned claw. Then it opened its jaws and the air around its muzzle dissolved in a shimmer of heat. The pistol began to melt. Dushma had to turn away as she felt her eyebrows singeing.

The clatter of train wheels could now be heard approaching from around the bend in the tunnel. The elidra raised its head, ears swivelling. The red-hot remains of the pistol spilled to the ground.

Though the oncoming train was still hidden from view, its headlamps lit up the curving tunnel wall. Dushma stumbled forward as if to make her way around the elidra, but it moved to block her path. Its eyes faded to a gentle yellow as it gazed at her, swaying its head from side to side uncertainly. Then it lowered itself down towards the floor of the tunnel, its haunches bunching as if ready to spring, its shoulders level with Dushma's face.

She hesitated. She wasn't sure if she had sufficient strength left.

A ripple ran through the elidra. Its tail thrashed with impatience. Its scales glowed and a comforting wave of warmth came from its body.

Dushma half fell, half jumped forward and somehow locked her arms around the elidra's neck. She flung one leg up over its back, her shoe scrabbling on the slippery metal surface. For a moment she was certain she would fall. Then she found a foothold on the elidra's serrated spine and managed to pull herself upright.

With a thunderous clap of wings the elidra launched itself into the air.

Looking over her shoulder, Dushma caught a glimpse of the front of the train as it turned the corner behind them. Then they had rounded another bend and were powering their way on down the dimly lit tunnel, the faint lights flickering past them in a steadily accelerating blur.

They joined a wider tunnel where two lines of track ran side by side. The elidra spread its pinions to their full extent and increased its speed yet more. Through its flexible metal skin Dushma could feel the squeeze of springs, the swing of counterweights and the punch and slide of pistons. She opened her mouth and tossed her head, her face whipped by her straggling hair. She had never moved this fast before.

A noise like a drumroll thundered in her ears. *We've gone through the sound barrier!* she thought. A fierce heat began to scorch the bare flesh of her calves.

They flew still faster but the noise didn't stop. Instead it receded and then doubled in volume in a sequence of numbing crescendos.

Burning shreds of debris swirled in the air beneath the elidra's wings. Twisting her head, Dushma saw a dirty orange balloon of flame swelling up along the tunnel towards them. *Gunpowder*, Beltrowser had said. *Tons of it*.

Her scalp prickled and her palms became slippery with sweat. She almost lost her grip as the elidra threw back its neck, angled its wings and began to climb.

The ceiling had opened out above them and they were ascending rapidly inside what looked like a brick-lined chimney. High overhead, Dushma saw a metal grille like the bottom of a sieve. Beyond it was the open sky, filled with dark banks of cloud. Across this patch of dull grey light circled three enormous triangular shadows.

They were in a ventilation shaft, rising towards the beating arms of the giant fan.

They rose faster and faster. Dushma felt as if weights were piling up inside her stomach, one for every beat of the elidra's wings. The walls of the ventilation shaft glowed red as the seething cloud of burning gas came after them.

They missed the fan by millimetres. The wake from the sweeping propeller blade nearly spilled them from the air. Thrashing its wings to regain its balance, the elidra climbed the short remaining distance to the metal grille that capped the ventilation shaft.

It tore at the grille with its teeth and claws, slicing the wire like string. Its neck swayed and flexed like the branch of a tree in a storm. Dushma squeezed her eyes tight shut and clung on with all her might. The hot air rising around them was painful in her lungs.

Its tail lashing from side to side, the elidra squeezed itself through the gap in the mesh. Ragged strands of wire snagged Dushma's clothing and for a moment she thought she would be ripped from the elidra's back.

Then with a rush they came tumbling out into the open air and over the lip of the ventilation shaft.

Two lofty brick columns rose up on either side of them. Below stretched the cityscape of narrow streets, chimneys and church spires that Dushma had known for as long as she could remember. They had emerged directly beneath her old home in the arch of the railway viaduct.

For a moment everything was perfectly calm. The elidra,

its wings scarcely moving, flew gently down through the early morning breeze. Dushma heard the sound of birdsong and felt soft raindrops wetting her face.

Then the top of the ventilation shaft blew off.

There was a roar like the sound of giant waves breaking on a stony beach. A geyser of burning gas swarmed in flaming coils up the walls of the viaduct. The fan was sheared from its axle and thrown spinning into the air, gouts of smoke belching after it. Glass cascaded from the shattered windows of nearby buildings.

The shock wave crumpled the elidra like a discarded chocolate wrapper. It tumbled head over heels through the smoke and Dushma lost her hold around its neck. She fell two or three metres and landed jarringly, rolling over several times. She came to rest on her hands and knees, hot bits of metal and brick pelting the ground around her.

There was now so much smoke in the air that she couldn't tell where she was. Flames could be seen here and there through the dense black clouds. She hunched into a protective ball, knees under her chin and arms shielding her head.

She lay with her eyes squeezed tightly shut for several minutes while the debris from the explosion continued to fall. When nothing had landed for a count of one hundred she uncurled herself, rose slowly to her feet and looked around.

A scene of total destruction was beginning to appear through the clearing smoke. Wrecked cars lay buckled and crushed in heaps, one on top of the other. Nearby was a telephone box on its side, lumps of concrete pavement still attached to its base. Filing cabinets were piled here and there, drawers spilling out beside them. There were ovens and fridges with the doors torn off and mangled bedsteads strewn among pyramids of empty oil drums.

At first Dushma simply stared in disbelief. Then she noticed the barbed wire fencing, the mobile crane on caterpillar tracks and the padlocked shed with the sign on top of it. The explosion had not, after all, caused a city-wide apocalypse. She was in a scrapyard.

A siren started up in the distance.

Dushma looked round for the elidra but it was nowhere to be seen. She could not even be sure if it had fallen or landed near her. The ground was too churned up for any claw marks to be visible.

She walked back and forth along the rutted tracks, searching between the mounds of scrap metal. She peered into cage-like tangles of iron bars and through the shattered windows of burnt-out vehicles, but saw no gleam of silvery scales among the rust and tarnish. "Hello!" she called out, her voice hoarse and cracking. "Where are you? Please…" She cocked her head to listen for the whirr of its motors or the metallic rustling of its wings, but all she heard was the scrape and creak of an old mattress spring moving in the wind.

At last, admitting defeat, she began to make her way towards the scrapyard gates. As she went she caught a glimpse of herself in the wing mirror of one of the derelict cars. She recoiled at the sight. What hair that hadn't been singed from her scalp stood up around her head in a blasted halo of frazzled black strands. Her face was scratched and her skin was caked with soot and grime. Dried blood from her cut lip stained her chin and her eyes were red and swollen. Her clothes hung from her body in rags. She looked like the ghost of an electrocuted corpse. She shuddered and glanced away.

A wooden handle protruded from the nearest pile of scrap. She seized it and pulled free one half of a pair of broken shears. Impulsively she began to hack at the remains of her hair with the rusty blade. Then she tore a strip from the sleeve of her blouse, wetted it with spit and tried to rub some of the dirt from her face.

When she had finished her hair was clumped in spiky quills around her head and her cheeks were blotchy and smeared. She weighed the half-pair of shears in her hand for a moment, wondering whether to take it with her. It was blunt but looked fearsome enough.

Instead she drew back her arm and drove the blade with all her might into the gravelly soil at her feet. It sank in to a depth of several centimetres and then stood upright, the handle quivering.

Reaching the entrance to the scrapyard, she found the gates unattended and unlocked. Pulling them a little way open she squeezed herself through the gap and out into the deserted street.

Her view no longer blocked by the mounds of scrap metal, she could see the viaduct again. The flames from the exploding ventilation shaft had taken hold and it was burning fiercely. Blazing pieces of wood and masonry were dropping from the underside of the arch. Plumes of smoke blackened the air. Dushma watched impassively for a little while, then turned away. The sound of sirens grew louder as the fire engines began to arrive.

Elsewhere the sky was clearing. The rain had stopped and a pale sun was becoming visible through the cloud. Across the city, windows, weathercocks, radio masts and cranes began to gleam in the watery light. Towering over all of them, its gargoyles and spires still emerging from the mist, stood St Gotha's Cathedral.

Raising her head defiantly and lifting up her tired feet, Dushma set out towards it.

About the Author

Patrick Wood was born in Leeds in 1968. As a boy he read everything he could lay his hands on, but wrote music rather than fiction. He studied mathematics in Oxford and London and is currently working as a software developer.

Electric Dragon is his first published novel.

Look out for the gripping fantastical
sequel to *Electric Dragon*…

FIREGLASS MACHINE

Fireglass. A mythical substance – indestructible,
almost alive. Its creation is said to require a grisly
sacrificial rite.

For Dushma, orphan and former fugitive, this legend is
just one more unpleasant memory of a life she wants to
leave behind. But the past is not so easily discarded. After
a terrifying nocturnal encounter, it gradually becomes
clear to her that the experiments of a long-dead alchemist
have been successfully re-enacted. A machine is out of
control beneath the streets of London, and this time the
sacrifice is still to be made.